Will the Rim-to-Rim

NOW THE TRAIL GOT TOUGHER, AND TESS WORKED HARD NOT to let her hopes and dreams fall onto the ground before her. The path grew steep and smooth from the feet of thousands of hikers. Tess's feet were almost straight up and down, her toes jammed into the rim of her new boots. But she kept up with Vince.

This is tough, but I am too. I will not fall behind. She began to jog. All of a sudden, the earth beneath her gave way. A large rock twisted out of the trail, twisting Tess's ankle with it.

"Oh no!" she cried out, as she slipped and fell. Her hip hit the ground so hard she thought she had landed on concrete.

"Tess, are you all right?" Her dad, only a few feet behind her, caught up with her quickly. Vince and the others had heard her fall and had turned around and come back to help. She looked up and tried to focus on the people around her.

Secret Sisters: (se′-krit sis′-terz) n. Two friends who choose each other to be everything a real sister should be: loyal and loving. They share with and help each other no matter what!

Secret Sisters

First Place

Sandra Byrd

WATERBROOK
PRESS

FIRST PLACE
PUBLISHED BY WATERBROOK PRESS
5446 North Academy Boulevard, Suite 200
Colorado Springs, Colorado 80918
A division of Random House, Inc.

ISBN 1-57856-066-7

Published in association with the literary agency of Janet Kobobel Grant, Books & Such, 3093 Maiden Lane, Altadena, CA 91001.

Library of Congress Cataloging-in-Publication Data

Byrd, Sandra.
First place / Sandra Byrd.—1st ed.
p. cm.—(The secret sisters series ; bk. 9)
Summary: Rivalries between the Secret Sisters and the Coronado Club surface and create problems at Outdoor School.
ISBN 1-57856-066-7
[1. Camps—Fiction. 2. Friendship—Fiction. 3. Christian life—Fiction.] I. Title.

PZ7.B9898 Fi 2000
[Fic]—dc21

99-047797

Printed in the United States of America
2000—First Edition

10 9 8 7 6 5 4 3 2 1

For Lisa Bergren and Janet Kobobel Grant,
friends, encouragers, and editors extraordinaire.
Without them, I couldn't run this particular race.

"Therefore, since we are surrounded
by such a huge crowd of witnesses
to the life of faith, let us strip off every weight
that slows us down.... And let us run
with endurance the race that God has set before us."
Hebrews 12:1, NLT

one

Boy Scouts

Early Wednesday Evening, May 14

"I haven't even started to pack yet. Have you?" Twelve-year-old Tess Thomas pushed her coffee brown hair behind her ears and shifted her legs on the bleachers. Lots of people were at the high school diamonds this evening, even in the heat, to watch the Babe Ruth Little League games. The burnt smell of grilled hot dogs drifted through the evening air.

Her best friend, Erin, smiled. "You know me. I have everything in my duffel bag. Outdoor School is going to be totally exciting. How can we wait two more days?"

Tess should have known Erin had packed. Probably ironed her stuff too, if Tess knew her Secret Sister as well as she thought she did. She smiled. Oh well, she would pack after the baseball game. Or tomorrow. "Do you want to move up higher where we'll have more shade?" she asked. The bleachers had a partial roof farther back.

"Okay." Erin leaned over toward her mother. "We're moving up out of the sun, okay?"

Mrs. Janssen nodded absent-mindedly from underneath

her straw hat and waved her hand, never taking her eyes off Erin's older brother, Tom, who was next up at bat. Tess wanted to watch him too. She hoped he would get a hit.

The girls settled farther back, and Erin fished a plastic bag out of her backpack.

"What's that?" Tess asked.

"Snacks."

Of course. Would Erin ever be without snacks?

"I brought Lemon Heads for you." Erin shook the Baggie in Tess's direction. "And friendship twists." Reaching into the bag, Erin pulled out some red licorice strings, which she looped into hearts, then pulled tight into knots before handing one to Tess. "See, a heart for our friendship, and a knot, which means it can't be undone!"

"Cool." Tess popped one into her mouth and then cheered loudly as Tom got a base hit.

The Arizona sun had worked overtime today, melting everything in sight. The school's asphalt driveway still stank of the tar-tinged steam it had leaked into the afternoon air.

Oh no! As Tess turned to set down her backpack, she noticed Lauren, the queen of the popular Coronado Club, sitting in the corner of the bleachers. A group of her cling-ons surrounded her. *Please have her leave us alone,* Tess prayed.

"Do you think the counselors will give us really hard things to do at Outdoor School?" Erin asked, her voice as calm as the breeze-free evening. Obviously, she hadn't seen Lauren yet.

"Like what?" Tess asked, forcing herself to ignore the Coronado Club. "I think it's just camping and cool stuff. I mean, it's supposed to be fun, a reward before graduating from sixth grade, and we sold all that candy to make sure we could go."

"I am so sick of chocolate. I never want to see any again!" Erin agreed. The sixth grade had sold candy as a fund-raiser for Outdoor School. Now that the work was done, all three classes couldn't wait to head to Flagstaff—and cool air—for four days of outdoor fun.

"Yeah, but it was worth it." Tess smiled. "Now we get cabin number one!" Cabin number one was the coolest at the camp, and the Secret Sisters and their friends, Katie and Joann, had slaved for weeks to sell enough candy to win that prize.

Tess chewed a hangnail before mentioning a topic she was beginning to dread. "But first I have to finish the Rim-to-Rim."

"It'll be fun! Don't worry. You can do it. Look how long you've been training with your dad."

"That's true," Tess admitted. She and her dad had been hiking up and down the desert mountains for months, preparing to walk from the South Rim to the North Rim of the Grand Canyon. They were leaving this Friday and hiking Saturday and Sunday. Outdoor School started Sunday night.

"It's just that my dad wants to be on the first-place team. It's really important to him. His company makes it into a contest. Whoever turns in the overall best time on both days of the hike wins some kind of prize. So everyone goes fast, and I'm kind of afraid they'll hike too fast for me."

"You can do it. I know you can!" Erin put her arm around her friend's shoulders for a second.

"I guess." Despite her training, Tess had troubling doubts about her ability to make it all the way. Especially now, although she hadn't told anyone why.

Tess heard a giggle behind her and turned just a little to look.

"What's up?" Erin asked when she saw Tess frown.

"Lauren and Colleen are a few rows behind us, up in the dark corner where it's hard to see them."

"You're kidding. What are they doing here?"

"Who knows?" Tess answered. "They're like poison oak. No matter what we do, we can't get rid of them." She paused and then added, "You know what I think? I think they're boy scouts."

Erin looked at her friend's face. "What are you talking about?"

"That's what Tyler calls certain girls in his class. They're out scouting for boys."

Erin cracked up, and Tess lost it too. They both laughed loudly.

Erin reached behind her to put away her snack bag. "Uh-oh," she said, as she turned back toward Tess.

"What?"

"They must have heard us."

Tess scooted closer and whispered, "Why do you say that?"

"Because Lauren and Colleen are heading our way."

two

The Challenge

Early Wednesday Evening, May 14

Lauren stood over Tess and Erin, staring down at them. Taking a long, noisy slurp on her soda, Lauren drained it before talking. "Hi, girls," she said, swooping down next to Erin. Red-haired Colleen sat on the other side of Tess.

"Hi," Tess answered, her voice flat. A bitter taste, like medicine, filled her mouth. For a while, nobody talked. Lauren pulled out a nail file and worked on her nails for a minute. She blew the nail powder into the air and admired all ten fingers before putting the file back into her fanny pack. Tess looked at her own bitten stubby nails and shoved them into her pockets.

"I hear your brother is on the other team," Lauren said, facing Erin. "Isn't he number fifteen?" She took a little crystal clip out of her sun-bleached hair and rearranged her hair.

"Yeah, he is," Erin said. "I take it you're here to cheer on the Panthers." The Panthers were the team playing—and currently beating—Erin's brother's team. It was nearly the end of the game.

"My dad is their coach." Lauren tossed her empty cup on the bleachers. "Your brother's a pretty good player."

"Yeah, and she thinks he's cute, too." Colleen giggled.

Lauren didn't say she agreed with that, but she didn't disagree either. She just sat there smiling sweetly into outer space.

Tess's face flushed, but she didn't look at either of them. So Colleen and Lauren *were* boy scouts! Nobody but Erin knew Tess had special feelings about Erin's older brother, Tom. Tess sure wasn't about to share that little fact with the Coronado Club.

"Well, it's too bad he's not on a good team. He *is* an excellent athlete." Lauren stared into the Cougars' dugout.

"He is. And he thinks Tess is an excellent athlete too. He said so last month," Erin answered.

Tess almost smiled. Leave it to good old Erin to defend both her brother and her best friend with one sentence.

Lauren turned toward Tess. "He said that?" she asked, as if she couldn't believe it.

Erin nodded, smiling, and then said, "Yeah, he did."

"And just what kind of sports do you participate in? Besides selling candy, I mean." Lauren sneered.

So *that* was it. Now Tess figured out why Lauren was being especially mean to them today. She was mad because the Coronado Club hadn't won cabin number one.

"I hike," Tess spoke up, her voice cracking only a little. She felt braver now that she knew what was going on.

"Oh, I see. Waaalking," Lauren said. She sniffed.

"Not just walking!" Erin stood up. Lauren stood up too, probably not wanting anyone to be taller than she was. "She's hiking all the way across the Grand Canyon this weekend. It's more than twenty miles of dangerous hiking. And besides, her team is going to finish in first place!"

"Wow, cool!" Colleen said and gave Tess a thumbs-up.

Tess smiled, glad to see some sign of friendship from Colleen. But Lauren shot a nasty look in Colleen's direction, and Colleen grew quiet.

"Well, that's quite a challenge," Lauren said. "I wouldn't count on making it, though. Kids hardly ever do. My cousin Melinda tried that hike two years ago when she was in tenth grade, and she had to ride a mule back because the walk was too hard."

"Maybe Melinda hadn't trained well enough," Tess said, standing up. Fat chance she was going to let Lauren intimidate her. Not again. Not this time.

"Oh, she trained plenty," Lauren said.

Colleen spoke up. "Isn't Outdoor School going to be fun?"

Looking at Colleen, Tess thought she had been nice to try to change the subject. Last summer she and Colleen had been best friends. Colleen had been fun and funny. But when Lauren came back from summer vacation, Colleen traded Tess in for Lauren. Colleen had kind of turned into a wimp since she had been back with Lauren, but now Colleen was practically interrupting Lauren. Strange.

"Yes," Erin said. "We can't wait! And I think it's really neat that you guys are in charge of the campfire entertainment each night."

This time Tess did smile. Even though Colleen and Lauren had been trying to make fun of Tess, Erin had found something nice to say about them. That's just how she was. And that's why she was the best Secret Sister ever.

"Yeah, it'll be fun," Colleen agreed. "Maybe we can do skits."

"Well, of course you two will have a good time," Lauren said, lip curling. "Now that you're staying in cabin number one. We should have gotten it, you know. We sold the most."

Cabin number one was the most private of all the cabins, with two sets of bunk beds, plus a twin for the counselor, while the other cabins had eight or ten bunks.

"What are you talking about?" Erin asked.

"Colleen, Melody, Andrea, and I sold more than you, Tess, Katie, and Joann. I asked Mr. Basil, and he said it was true."

Mr. Basil, the sixth-grade teacher in charge of Outdoor School, wouldn't lie about that. But Mrs. Rodriguez, Tess and Erin's teacher, had told them that cabin number one was theirs. Tess felt a lump of concern drop into her throat. What if the cabin wasn't theirs after all?

"Mrs. Rodriguez told us that we won," Erin said.

"That's true," Colleen agreed. "We didn't hand our money in on time because Melody was on vacation."

Tess had noticed Melody hadn't sat at the Coronado Club table at lunch all week. Lauren must have been punishing her.

"I'm sorry you didn't turn your money in on time," Tess said. "But we did earn the cabin fair and square." *Besides, Lauren's daddy bought a case of candy,* she thought. *Lauren's dad always is trying to buy her way out of everything. That's not fair either.*

Tess felt the pressure on her heart as the Lord urged her to think kind thoughts and not mean ones. *Sorry, Jesus. I'm glad you helped me not to say that out loud.* Just because Lauren was snobby didn't mean Tess needed to be.

"Well, Miss First Place," Lauren continued, "let's just

see how sure you are that you can win the Rim-to-Rim. Since we're choosing the campfire activities for the first night, I think you should bring your blue ribbon. We'll have you stand up and tell about your hike. How you made it—or how you didn't."

No one spoke.

"Unless," Lauren added, "you aren't so sure you're going to make it. I mean, you *are* a good athlete, right?"

"I'll make it. Don't worry," Tess said. "But—"

Erin interrupted. "She's an awesome hiker. She'll definitely take first place."

"Good, then it's settled." Lauren half smiled at Tess and Colleen. "I'll start to spread the word at school tomorrow that you'll be ready to tell everyone all the little details of your grand disaster—I mean, grand adventure—on Sunday night."

Colleen opened her mouth as if to say something, but Lauren gave her a bruising look, turned on her heel, and began to step from row to row over the bleachers on the way down to the Panthers' dugout. Colleen looked at Tess with regret but said nothing, following Lauren instead. Erin looked at Tess, who stared back. But neither of them spoke.

three

Secret Sisters Forever

Wednesday Evening, May 14

"Oh, great, now what am I going to do?" Tess ran her hands through her hair and held them there for a minute. She felt like pulling it out in frustration. People were milling around the bleachers as the game began to wind down.

"What do you mean, what are you going to do? You're going to hike, you're going to make it, and you'll finish first too." Erin put her arm around Tess, but Tess shook it off.

"It's just not that simple!"

"Why not? You've trained right. You've run up and down Camelback Mountain dozens of times. Same with Squaw Peak and South Mountain. You're an awesome athlete. I really mean it. Tom thinks so too." Erin's caramel-colored hair looked almost brown in the growing shadows.

The day slipped behind the horizon now, and as the dark crept across the baseball field, the lights shone brightly for the final inning.

"Besides, so what if you don't win? I mean, you don't care what the Coronado Club thinks of you anymore, right?" Erin said.

"I care about telling the whole sixth grade."

"It'll be totally great. A lot of people admire you for hiking in the Rim-to-Rim. They'll love to hear it. It'll take maybe five minutes, and then it'll be over."

Yeah, if I win. Or even make it, Tess thought, but she said nothing.

"You're going to be great. I know you'll do everything you set out to do. And I'll stand next to you at the campfire that night so you won't feel like a dweeb up there all by yourself."

"Really?" Tess asked.

"Really," Erin said. "Secret Sisters forever, right?"

Tess smiled. "Right!"

The game was over, and the players headed off the field. The Panthers had won, unfortunately. As the teams started to slap one another's hands, saying "Good game," Erin zipped up her backpack. Tess slipped her feet back into her sandals. They stepped over the bleachers, walking to meet Erin's mom, who was talking with a friend. A cloud of chalky smoke hung in the air as boys beat the bases to rid them of dust before packing them into the team rucksacks.

"We'll meet you at the car, okay?" Erin said. Her mother nodded. The girls walked in silence.

"You still seem kind of worried," Erin said.

"Oh, not really." *Why don't I just tell her?* Tess asked herself.

"Hi, Erin. Hi, Tess." Tom walked over and put his equipment into the back of the Suburban. He peeled off his batting glove and stuffed it inside his baseball mitt, then slammed the car's back door.

"Hi, Tom." Tess smiled at him. "Good game."

"Thanks. We lost though."

"Yeah, but you played okay," Erin said. "Still, would you please sit in the front with Mom? You stink." She plugged her nose, and her brother walked over and gave her a big hug.

"P-U," she said, moving away.

"Okay, you three, hop into the car," Mrs. Janssen said as she climbed into the car and started the engine. "You all ready for your hike?" She turned around and smiled at Tess.

"Yes," Tess answered. The dark streets flew by on the way to her house, and she rolled down her window, letting the breeze blow over her sweaty forehead. She looked at Erin's mother, at Tom, and finally at Erin. They believed in her, and she believed in herself, right?

"I'm home." Tess kicked off her sandals, watching with satisfaction as they flew directly into the shoe basket inside the tiled front hallway. She heard the familiar rustle of the newspaper in the family room, and a strange buzzing noise from the kitchen. She headed toward the buzz.

"Hey, old girl, you're just in time for the first legal scalping this century." Tess's brother, Tyler, sat in a kitchen chair with a towel draped around his shoulders.

"What's going on?"

"Brain a bit dull this evening? Mum's on a new money-saving kick, and I'm the first victim."

Tess smiled at her brother, with his silly, lovable British accent. Tyler had a one-track mind, that was for sure. He wanted to be a detective like his heroes on public television, most of whom were from England. He constantly practiced talking like them.

"Cutting hair at home now?" Tess said, reaching up to touch her own tresses. She already had experienced one high-risk haircut this year, after her twelfth birthday. That one was okay, but she didn't know about her mom cutting her hair.

"Hi, honey." Mrs. Thomas, her tummy huge with a growing baby, kissed her daughter on the cheek. Then she turned on the buzzer and went back toward Tyler's head. "Only the guys. I don't trust myself on girls' hair yet. It's harder. But we can save twenty dollars a month if I do Tyler's and Dad's this way." She sheared a piece off of the back of Tyler's head.

"Discrimination! I say if you do the boys, you do the girls!"

"I'd be careful how you talk to Mom when she has a weapon in her hand," Tess said.

As if to prove the point, Mrs. Thomas revved the buzzer motor and took another slim strip of hair off Tyler's scalp.

"Now, now, let's be careful. I say, I don't want my head to look like a bull's-eye from behind!" Tyler reached around and felt the back of his head.

"You won't. I promise," his mom said. "Don't you know anyone else whose mom cuts his hair?"

"No. Uh, wait. I think Jeremy got a haircut like this before he went in for his brain surgery. His brain recovered, but his hair never did."

Tess laughed and winked at her brother. "You must be growing up. I never knew you were so concerned about how you looked!"

"Got an image to maintain, old girl."

Mrs. Thomas scooted around the chair and lopped off another band of Tyler's hair. "Tess, could you go in and tell Dad to get ready to be 'scalped' in about five minutes?"

"Okay." Tess grabbed an apple and picked up her backpack from the kitchen floor. She was thankful she had very little homework tonight.

"Hi, Dad." She sat down on the couch. "Mom says get ready for your haircut in five minutes."

Her dad rolled his eyes. "I'll be glad when this baby is born and the crazy ideas stop popping into her head. Of course, if the haircut looks bad, maybe Vince will think we're poor and give me a raise."

"Is Vince all ready for the Rim-to-Rim?" Tess asked.

"Oh yeah. He's really ready. And he's amazed that my twelve-year-old daughter is ready too. I told him, look out. She'll probably lead the team!"

Runaway nerves twitched inside of Tess's stomach.

"Jim," her mother called from the other room, "no stalling! You're next."

"I'd better go, cupcake. And you had better do your homework." Mr. Thomas folded his newspaper and set it on the family room floor. He tousled Tess's hair as he left the room.

Tess rolled down the cuff of her sock.

She ran her fingers over her right ankle. It throbbed lightly, like a pulse, in response to the pressure. Nobody knew that the injury she received last January when she had tried out for gymnastics might be back. Probably from the hiking she was doing to prepare for the Rim-to-Rim. A few days ago she thought she had noticed a little swelling. It wasn't painful, really. Just...noticeable.

four

High Siders

Thursday Afternoon, May 15

"Hi, Mozart." As Tess walked in the house, she waved to her brother, who was already pounding the piano keys. Apparently he had raced home from school to finish his practice time because he had something exciting to do that afternoon.

Next to the piano bench sat Hercules, Tyler's pet horned toad, in his glass cage. Tess cut through the living room to the kitchen and stopped to look at Hercules. Gross. His eyes rolled all the way around in their sockets. She looked at Tyler and suppressed a giggle. His haircut did look kind of geeky. She ran her hand along the stiff back fuzz as she passed by.

"Move on, old girl," Tyler said, not missing a note.

She walked into the kitchen.

"How was your day?" Mrs. Thomas asked.

"Fine," Tess said. "Hi, baby." She patted her mother's tummy, which was sticking way out these days. The baby moved beneath Tess's hand.

"The baby always moves when Tyler plays the piano. I think he or she likes to hear him."

"Well, that's one person in the family then," Tess teased.

"Now, Tess..."

"Oh, Mom, you know I love the 'old fruit.' And he can play really well. But why is he practicing so early?"

"I'm driving him to Big Al's house in half an hour. They're taking him out for pizza since he'll be gone this weekend. He's leaving Hercules at Al's house while we're away. Say, that reminds me." She took a head of lettuce out of the fridge and peeled off the protective plastic. "Are you packed?"

"Uh, sort of."

"Yes, I know what that means: You have a bunch of stuff stacked on your dresser that you might want to wear and another pile of dirty clothes on the floor that needs to be washed."

"Exactly!" Tess said, making herself a peanut butter and jelly sandwich. It always amazed her how hungry she was after school. After all, it wasn't like lunch was that long ago. Must be brainwork. "I'll get at it in a minute," she said, scraping a hunk of gooey white bread off the roof of her mouth with her tongue. "Do we have any milk?"

"Yes. Go ahead and pour yourself some. Then get busy," her mother said.

Tess drank her milk then went into her bedroom.

"Yep. Stacks all over. Piles all over. Hi, Goldy." Tess tapped the goldfish bowl and dumped in about a tablespoon of fish food. "That should last you."

As she passed her bed, she walked by her Bible. *Haven't spent much time with you lately,* she thought guiltily. *I'd better do it now. Sorry, Lord.*

As she picked up her Bible, she saw the Sports Outlet catalog underneath. She had taken that from the Sunday paper. *I guess it's been four days since I read my Bible. Not so good.*

She opened up to John, which her Sunday school class was reading. But her thoughts wandered from the Word. What could she do about her ankle?

Now her mind was completely off the Bible and on her problem. What about the Sports Outlet catalog? Maybe there was something helpful in it. Like a bandage or something. So much for a chapter. She had read only one verse. But she had important problems to solve. She stuck her bookmark in at the same place as before, snapped her Bible shut, and hurried to her desk.

She thumbed through the pages of the Sports Outlet ad. "No, not bicycles. Aha, this is it! New hiking boots—'High Siders'! With these I'll have all the support I need and do just fine. And they're on sale this week. It must be a message from God to me. I'll buy new boots."

She ripped out that page of the ad and went to ask her mother.

"Absolutely not," her mom said. "No way. We're already spending a fortune on this trip, what with staying overnight and eating out. You saw me cutting Tyler's and Dad's hair last night. That wasn't just for fun, dear. We don't have a lot of extra money." Her mother set the salad bowl back into the fridge to wait for dinner and ran a dishcloth over the countertop.

"But, Mom, I need them. I really do. This is an emergency, and I don't see why you can't understand that!" Tess pleaded. "This really is an emergency. I have to make first place."

"Tess, you might not make first place anyway, honey. You need to think about that. A lot of experienced hikers are going out this weekend."

"But Dad plans to win. And I need new boots."

"Your hiking boots aren't that old. Dad didn't say you needed new ones."

Tess plopped down at the kitchen table. If she told her mom her ankle hurt, her mom might overreact and make Tess cancel the hike altogether. Her options were running out. This called for drastic measures.

"What if I pay for them myself?"

"That's a lot of money."

"I know. But I worked hard to earn it." It was true. She hadn't planned to spend money now, but…

Her mother sighed. Tess felt a teeny bit sorry for annoying her mother, who was already stressed with her pregnancy and her writing work and all, but Tess couldn't help it.

"All right. Be ready to go in twenty minutes when I take Tyler to Al's. We're going to Sports Outlet but nowhere else. If they don't have them, too bad."

"Thanks, Mom. You're the best!" Of course they would have them. It was the perfect solution.

Half an hour later they arrived at Big Al's to drop off Tyler. Big Al came running out of the house to meet them. "Hey, Tess, I hear you're going to hike the canyon. Maybe it'll take a couple of pounds off." Big Al was so obnoxious. It was his main occupation.

"Then maybe you ought to come along, huh, Al?" Tess said. She caught a disapproving look from her mother and said nothing else.

They drove off.

"Tess, you know better than that."

"I know, Mom. I'm sorry. But he started it!"

"Yes, and you're older and should be wiser. Or at least kinder."

Her mother jerked the car to a stop just as the light turned red. She had almost run that light. Tess didn't say anything aloud though. This wasn't the time. "I suppose," was all she said. She didn't want to think about whether her mother was right or not. She just wanted her new shoes.

Five minutes later they pulled into Sports Outlet, and Tess hopped out of the Jeep. The shock of moving from the air-conditioned car to the scorching, 100-degree heat felt as though she were leaping into an oven.

"Let's get inside," her mother said. They hurried into the store.

"I'll meet you in five minutes. I'm going to buy Dad a new hat and bandanna. Do you need either of those?" her mother asked.

"I have a hat but not a good bandanna."

"All right. I'll pick one up."

Tess strode over to the shoe area and searched the racks for the High Siders. "Size five," she muttered, as she looked over the selection. "What am I, Cinderella?"

Finally. Stuffed way in the back, in a half-crushed box, she found one pair of size-eight High Siders. "All right! Thanks, Lord." She took them out and tried them on. Perfect.

She would definitely do some awesome hiking in these boots. And just to make sure she didn't get blisters from new shoes, she grabbed a pack of moleskin to pad around her socks.

She wore the shoes to meet her mom. She would walk in them all day today and tomorrow. Surely that would break them in.

"Ready to go? Do those feel okay?" her mom asked.

"Yes!" Tess said, taking out her wallet and unpeeling some of the bills she carefully had been saving from babysitting money.

The only problem was, even with these boots on, her ankle still throbbed just the tiniest bit. But that would probably go away soon.

five

Let's Go!

Friday Afternoon, May 16

The next afternoon was filled with rushing, packing, planning, talking, and jamming things into the car. Now only a few more minutes remained until they left.

The phone rang yet again.

"Telephone, madam," Tyler said, rolling his eyes. This was the third phone call for Tess in the last twenty minutes.

"Hello?"

"Hi," said a voice.

"Joann?"

"Hi!" said another voice.

"Katie?"

"We're on three-way calling," Joann said. "We both wanted to say good luck."

"Now, Joann, you know that Tess doesn't believe in luck, right?" Katie said.

"I'll take your good thoughts and prayers," Tess said.

"I can't remember the last time I prayed," Joann said. "But I'll think about it. Anyway, I know you can do it. You've been practicing a long time, and you're in awesome shape."

"I'll be thinking about you," Katie said. "And we'll save the softest bunk at cabin one for you since we know how tired you'll be." Her voice always sounded so cheerful; Tess knew Katie really meant what she said.

"We'll be right there in the front for the opening night campfire, ready to hear all about it," Joann said.

"Roasted marshmallows and a first-place ribbon. Yeah!" Katie added.

"I'll be there." Tess's mouth grew dry.

"Okay, well, see you later. Bye!"

After hanging up, Tess ran to her room to grab her suitcase and backpack.

"Whoa!" This was no ordinary backpack. Tess groaned under the weight of all she had put in it. The seams practically were bursting, trying to contain several pairs of thick cotton socks, polka dots of moleskin to prevent blisters, a bathing suit, lightweight shorts and T-shirts, a wind-resistant jacket, a bandanna, and trail mix. What could come out? She unpacked her Bible. It was so heavy. She would read it when she got home.

"Ready to go?" her dad called from the other room.

"Ready." Tess lugged her gear down the hall and into the garage. A few minutes later, the Jeep was packed, and they all climbed in.

"Put on your seat belt, Tyler," his mother said, as she snapped her own in place. Mr. Thomas started the car, backed it out, and they were off toward the Janssens' house just a few miles away.

"I wish I could hike with you guys," Tyler said.

"Maybe in a few years, buddy," his dad answered. "Your mom has some fun things planned for the two of you while Tess and I are hiking. Don't worry."

"I'm not really interested in staring into the big hole for two days."

"That 'big hole' is one of the wonders of the world!" his mother replied. She smiled. "And that's not all I have planned. You'll see."

It didn't take long to reach Erin's house. When they arrived, Tom was out front loading stuff into their Suburban.

"We're almost ready!" he said. He shoved the last bag into the back, then slammed the door shut before the items could fall out onto the driveway. Soon the rest of his family came out and got into their car. Although they weren't hiking, Erin's family was joining Tess's for sightseeing and vacation. Then Sunday night the families would leave the girls at Outdoor School before returning home to Scottsdale.

Both cars headed toward the highway and north to their great adventure. Mile upon mile of desert rolled past Tess's window as she stared at the almost empty, sandy landscape. Soon miles of Teddy Bear cacti and floppy paloverde trees—alive with humming roaches—grew into stubby mountains and then larger ones. These mountains weren't peaked; they were mesas. The color of sawdust, their rugged, flat tops looked like a marine's new haircut.

About halfway to Grand Canyon Village, Tess's dad stopped for fuel and snacks. He pulled into a minimart and parked, and Erin's dad, following behind, did the same. It was still very hot. Tess hoped it would be cooler when they finally reached the Grand Canyon.

Josh, Erin's nine-year-old brother, came over to the Thomases' Jeep. Erin followed close behind.

"Want to trade?" Josh asked Tyler, as they all got out and stretched.

"Sisters, you mean? No, thanks. I already know how to handle this one."

Josh laughed. "No! I mean, do you want to ride with us? Erin and Tess could ride with your mom and dad. I don't know about you, but I'm totally bored. Then you and I could play Game Boys, if we want. My mom says it's okay with her."

"All right, old boy. Jolly good idea. Mom, is that okay?" Tyler asked his mother.

"Sure."

Soon Erin and her backpack were heading toward the Jeep.

"This is great!" she whispered to Tess.

Tess gave her a thumbs-up, and they climbed into the backseat.

"I suppose you have snacks in there," Tess whispered to Erin, pointing to Erin's backpack.

"But of course! Are you hungry?"

"No, not really." Tess didn't say anything else for a few minutes. She crossed her ankles, careful to put her right ankle on top so it wouldn't have any pressure on it.

"Do you have some paper in there?" she asked.

"Yep. Want a piece?"

Tess nodded, and Erin dug out a notebook with a neat cover. Tess's notebook, if she had thought to bring one, would probably have the cover ripped off. Or, if it was still on, it would be practically black with a tangle of scribbles. She grabbed the notebook and the offered pen and wrote: "I have something to tell you. But you have to promise not to say anything. Okay?"

She handed the notebook to Erin and glanced at her parents to see if they noticed anything. They were talking together and didn't even look in the backseat. Okay so far.

"Sure, what is it?" Erin wrote back.

"I have a little problem. I want you to pray about it with me. Do you remember when I was trying out for gymnastics last winter and I twisted my ankle on Squaw Peak?"

She handed the notebook to Erin.

Erin read it and looked with wide eyes at Tess. But she said nothing. "Yeah?" She scribbled back.

"Well, it's kind of back. I mean, not totally. But it's a little swollen, and it's not going down. If I poke my finger into it, it doesn't really hurt, but it kind of moves a little, feels like a heartbeat. I don't think it'll be a big deal, but I want you to pray that everything will be okay."

"All right. Are you sure you should still hike?" Erin wrote back.

"Yes!!" Tess wrote, underlining the word twice. " 'Cause it doesn't even hurt. But you know, twenty miles of the Grand Canyon is still a long way. So please pray, okay?"

"Okay." Erin wrote and drew a heart next to it with "SSF" inside for "Secret Sisters Forever."

Out of the front seat came her dad's voice. "Tess?"

She snapped shut the notebook. "Yeah, Dad?"

"I forgot to tell you something wonderful. Today at work Vince told us that the prize for first place is a hot-air-balloon ride. Isn't that great? I've always wanted to go on one, but they're so expensive. Just think, cupcake, soon you and I will be seeing the world from thousands of feet above the earth."

"Great, Dad, really," Tess said, swallowing what felt like a lump of clay in her throat. She didn't know why he was so certain they were going to win. Some of these people had already done this trip.

Erin reached over and squeezed her hand, hard. Tess squeezed back. She was glad Erin was in on the secret now. They could both pray about it.

six

Grand Canyon Village

Friday Evening, May 16

About an hour and a half later both cars pulled into Grand Canyon Village, the tiny town just outside of the park. Several hotels, restaurants, and mom-and-pop grocery stores dotted the main street. Tess's dad pulled into the Steak House.

"Anybody hungry?" he asked.

"Yes!" they all answered.

"Good. We need to get our energy up for tomorrow's hike. And those vacationers who aren't hiking still need something too!" He winked at Tess's mom, who rolled her eyes. They got out of the car and waited for Erin's family and Tyler.

I hope my family doesn't start to eat before they pray, Tess thought. *I should have warned them.*

Tess had become a Christian last October, after becoming friends with Erin, who had shared her faith with Tess. But her mom, dad, and brother still weren't Christians. Tyler had shown interest, asking questions and praying. He had even gone to church with her a few times. But her mom and dad? That was another story. Her mom seemed not to care one way or the other, but her dad had seemed opposed to Christianity. He had been strangely quiet on the subject for at least a month. Her prayer almost every day was that everyone in her family would become a Christian.

Both families walked up a wooden plank and into the restaurant. Pretend ponies, fashioned out of long bales of hay, lined the hallway, with well-worn saddles tossed over them. The hostess, sporting a sequined ranch shirt and Wrangler jeans, grabbed a handful of menus and walked up to them.

"How many this evening?" she asked.

"How many do we have?" Erin's dad was in front. He counted them. "Nine?"

"Yes, nine," his wife agreed. The hostess led them to a long table in the center of the room. Erin sat on one side of Tess, and Tess's mother sat on the other. Tom and Tyler and Josh sat facing them. Tyler had chosen to settle in between Tom and Josh. Tess smiled. She knew Tyler looked up to Tom and really liked being Josh's friend.

Erin asked, "Don't you think this is a little gross?" She pointed at the tablecloth. Tess looked at the white covering with long black ovals. Cowskin print. "Yuck. Especially since we're eating beef. I mean, it could have been this cow!"

"It's plastic, girls," Tom said. "I'm ordering beef!"

Tess's mother handed Tess a sheet of paper to pass along to Tyler. "Here's your menu," Mrs. Thomas said.

"I have a menu," he replied.

"I want you to order off this menu," she said. Tyler got up and walked around the table to whisper in his mother's ear. Tess was close enough to hear.

"But I don't *want* to order off the buckaroo menu," he pleaded. "Come on! It will be so embarrassing."

"Josh, you need to order off the buckaroo menu too," Josh's mom said.

"Oh, great, two buckaroos," Tyler complained, but he returned to his seat grinning. Tess guessed it wasn't so hard if you weren't the only buckaroo.

"I feel kind of sick. I don't want to eat anything," Josh said.

"I'm having the Cowgirl," Tess said. "Cowprint table-cloth or not."

"Me, too," Erin agreed.

Soon the waitress brought out huge steel bowls of salad for them to help themselves from, as if they were one, big family. *That's just how it is,* Tess thought. *My family and my Christian family. I wish we were all a Christian family.*

Just as Tess's dad was about to fork some salad into his mouth, Erin's dad said, "Is it all right with everyone if we pray before our meal?"

Tess held her breath. Her dad didn't answer, but he set down his fork. Everyone held hands while Erin's dad prayed. "Lord, thank you for this safe trip and this food and this friendship. We especially pray for Jim and Tess as they hike over the next two days, and we ask you to bless their efforts. May everything turn out for the best. In Jesus' name, amen."

Tess sighed and dug into the crisp, cold salad with a creamy ranch coating. The rest of the meal—grilled steaks and bowls heaped with pinto beans that were covered with a rich brown liquid—soon appeared. No one spoke much. Everyone just ate.

After the meal, Tyler asked to be excused to go to the

rest room. When he came back, he was laughing. "Guess what the sign over the bathroom said?" he asked Tom.

Please, Lord, nothing too embarrassing, Tess prayed.

"What?" Tom asked.

"Don't squat on yer spurs!"

The boys were laughing hard, but Tess was mortified. Didn't he have any manners? It all came from hanging out with Big Al. She elbowed her mother and gave her a pleading look.

"All right, Tyler, that's enough. If we're all done eating, we should be on our way."

They paid and headed toward the cars. On the way out, Tess noticed the sign hanging over the door. "Happy trails to you," it said cheerfully. She sincerely hoped her trails for the next two days would be happy ones.

An hour later they arrived at the Grand Canyon Park, checked into Bright Angel Lodge, and went outside to view the canyon. The Grand Canyon never failed to amaze Tess. But now that she had to hike—and sometimes run—across its enormous span, she thought the place looked both scary and pretty. The huge hollow in the ground covered several hundred square miles, layer upon layer of God-made earth, topped with limestone. Soft, sour-cream clouds lumped along the blue sky, which first turned salmon, and then purple, as the night settled in. The miles of pink peaks and rough, sandy-colored rocks looked ready to crumble into the canyon, many miles below. But they didn't. It was amazing how they had hung on for hundreds of years, just as they were.

"Isn't it a miracle?" Erin asked. She and Tess sat on a small wooden bench in front of Bright Angel Lodge.

"I was just thinking that," Tess said. "And feeling kind

of bad. I've had so much on my mind this week, I've kind of squeezed God out. I never made time for him. And now, when the hike is about to start, suddenly I'm begging him to help me even though I ignored him all week."

"I know. I do that too. But I think he understands. Maybe he's waiting for us right now," Erin said.

"Yeah. I feel him here with us."

"I brought my little Bible," Erin said. "Do you want me to read some?"

"Okay," Tess said, frowning.

"What's the matter?"

"I feel guilty. You brought your Bible, and I tossed mine out of my backpack because it was too heavy."

"Well, you're hiking, and I'm not. It's not like I'm Miss Perfect. I didn't take my Bible with me when we went to San Diego, but you did."

"That's true," Tess agreed. "That's why we're a team."

"I'll read the Sunday school verses in John," Erin said, turning to John 15. "'The greatest love a person can show is to die for his friends. You are my friends if you do what I command you.'"

The silent night settled quickly, and Tess knew she would have to go in soon. "Do you think you would die for your friends?"

"I don't know. I really love my friends and family, but dying?" Erin answered.

"I know. But it doesn't seem like Jesus asks very many people to die for him."

"Sometimes he does," Erin said. "But not too often."

"Maybe he just wants us to do other really hard things for him and for other people," Tess said.

"Yeah, I think so," Erin answered. A little boy ran by,

chasing his cowboy hat, which had blown from his head in the light wind.

"That reminds me," Tess said. "I forgot my hat, and I'm really going to need it for the hike. I suppose I have to spend more of my money to buy one. We had better get to the gift shop while it's still open."

Erin stood up and tucked her Bible into the zippered pocket of her fanny pack. "You can borrow mine, if you want."

"That would be great!"

Erin grinned. "You'll look like a neon orange, but if you get lost, people can find you."

"Thanks. But I hope I don't get lost! I mean, I'll stay on the trail. It's making it—and winning—that I'm worried about, you know, for my dad's sake. Not getting lost."

"Just teasing," Erin said. "I won't see you in the morning since you're going pretty early, so I'll say good-bye now." She hugged Tess. "I'll be praying for you. And don't worry. Everything is going to be just fine. I'm sure of it. I'll be waiting for you with the victory party on the other side Sunday afternoon." The nonhikers were staying at the South Rim Saturday night, too, then meeting the hikers Sunday on the North Rim.

Tess hugged Erin back and said good-bye.

The two girls walked into the lodge and went to their own families' rooms. Later that night, when Tess was in the shower, Erin must have come by and left the hat with Tess's mother. Tess got out of the shower and combed her wet hair, slipping into her lightweight sweats as pajamas before stepping back into the room with her family. As she did, she noticed the hat and picked it up off the bed. Tucked inside were the tiny pocket Bible and a licorice friendship knot.

seven

They're Off!

Saturday Morning, May 17

The next morning, Tess woke up at seven, but her dad was gone already. A few minutes after she had dressed, he came back into the room.

"Are you ready?" he asked.

Tess finished pulling her hair into a ponytail and fished it through the hole in the back of Erin's cap. She had on the layers—shorts and T-shirt with a sweatshirt over them—that the ranger had recommended. She gently pulled thick socks over the injured ankle, hoping to protect it even more.

"Yes." She grabbed her backpack and went to kiss her mother good-bye. "Where have you been?" she asked her dad.

"Checking on our gear, getting everything ready, talking with some of the others. But the Bright Angel Café is open now."

"I'll see you tomorrow, honey," her mother said. "You be careful and do a good job. Don't go too fast. You know Dad will slow down if you need to." She looked at her husband. He came back into the room to kiss her good-bye as well.

"Don't worry. We'll be fine. And Tess will probably set the pace. You'll see!" he said.

They said good-bye to a groggy Tyler, who rolled over in bed for the occasion, before falling back to sleep. Then they were off to the café for breakfast.

The tables were packed already, and the smell of pancakes drifted through the air.

"I'll have the hiker's breakfast," Tess ordered. Her dad had the same, with some coffee. In just a few minutes they had eaten the granola with warm milk, bananas, and blueberries. Now to meet the rest of the group from her dad's work, who were gathering at the mule corral in front of Bright Angel Trail. Tess pushed her nervous thoughts to the back of her mind, but they refused to obey and stay there.

The wranglers saddled up the mules, getting them ready to haul passengers and packs down the narrow pathways beaten into the canyon. "A mule ride might be kind of fun," she said to her dad.

"More fun to hike down," her dad said. "But the mules do have the right-of-way, so if some come up to us while we're hiking, we'll have to step to the side and let them pass. I'm hoping everyone will be here soon and we can beat this set of mules to the trails."

By eight o'clock, everyone had assembled, and they were ready to start. Four teams of hikers were going from her dad's job. Tess looked around. They were mostly men, with a couple of teenagers. One—no, two women were hiking with the teams. Tess smiled. She was the youngest one there.

The pungent smell of mule droppings mixed with the cool, fresh morning air, making the day seem both sweet and sour. The dew was thick on the rock walls, dripping like raindrops. Or teardrops.

"Hey, everybody, let's get going and talk about the rules here." Vince, her dad's boss, stepped to the front of their little group, and everyone gathered closer.

"Each of the four teams has the same number of hikers to start with, although it's fine to switch places as the hike gets underway, if you feel you can catch up with someone ahead of you. You must hike in groups of at least two. We're keeping track of two times. From here to Phantom Ranch today, and from Phantom Ranch to the lodge on the North Rim tomorrow. Best time of those two added together wins. No excuses."

Tess, her dad, and the others on her team stepped lively. Bright Angel trailhead beckoned in the crisp morning air, and she was ready to take it on. She could do it.

"This seems easy!" she said to her dad, as they practically jogged down the trail. The trail and the stone surrounding it were wheat colored, and thin streams of powder trickled down the trail before blowing as dust in the light wind. They passed through the stone cutout called Angels' Door and headed toward the greater trail. Ahead of them, Tess could see, the landscape changed. The trail looked smoother and a little greener. Pretty soon they would be deep in the belly of the canyon. Rocks the color of pennies leaned against one another and against the canyon walls.

Some were long and lean, some short and stubby. They looked like a bunch of gossiping girls.

They remind me of the Coronado Club, Tess thought. *Won't they be surprised when I get the first-place ribbon!*

Tess's team was leading, at first by only ten or fifteen minutes. Then their jogging put nearly half an hour between them and the others who were still easily visible on the trail behind them. Her ankle didn't hurt at all. The conversation among Tess, her dad, Vince, and Danny, the other guy on their team, swirled around them, giggles and jokes and teasing, as they threaded their way through the canyon majesty down toward the bottom. They wound around the switchbacks called Jacob's Ladder, which looped around and around the terrain like Christmas ribbon candy.

"There's a Bible story about Jacob's Ladder," Tess told her dad.

"Really?" he asked. "What is it?"

"A man named Jacob had a dream. In the dream a long ladder reached to heaven, with angels going up and down."

"You think it's that easy to get into heaven?" her dad asked.

"Easier," Tess replied. Her dad's expression changed, and she didn't say any more.

"Ready to refill the water?" Vince asked as they reached Indian Gardens, about four or five miles into the hike. "I don't want anyone getting dehydrated or having a heatstroke or anything else. Let's be smart hikers."

Oh, better finish my water. I haven't been paying attention. And refill it too.

They all sat for a few minutes, catching their breath. Tess bit into a Fuji apple, her favorite.

"Let's gear up!" her dad called a minute or two later. "Don't want to lose our lead!" The team hit the trail, Tess side by side with her father. She looked at her watch as her dad looked at his. They looked at each other and smiled. They were making very good time so far.

eight

A Twist

Saturday Morning, May 17

The easy times didn't last long, however. From far away, the trail had seemed to straighten out, but now that she was on it, Tess could see that it was as tricky and difficult as ever. Although the Jacob's Ladder switchbacks were behind them, plenty of challenges were here and now. Pits were in the earth where runaway rocks had bombed the trail, and the walk seemed to go around and around but never get anywhere.

"Doing okay?" her dad asked.

"Yes," she said, not liking to talk. She was saving energy instead. Sandstone crumbled down the canyon walls. Tess wasn't sure what kind of rock the earth beneath her feet was made of, but she could feel every muscle stretch. The ground was hard, and it pounded beneath her heels and the pads of her feet. They throbbed. Every step worked her muscles deeper and harder. Dust kicked up as she walked; it coated her mouth like gritty lipstick. When she opened her mouth, it powdered her tongue, too, like chalk.

"Just a couple more miles till Phantom Ranch!" her dad

called out cheerfully. She was in front of him; he wanted to walk behind her for safety. But Vince and the rest of their team were striding ahead. No matter how fast Tess walked, she seemed to fall farther behind them, drifting back like a balloon with a slow leak.

"I can do all things," she kept repeating, "through Christ, who gives me strength." Like the blood-colored rock around her, she needed to be tough to hold up. She clenched her teeth. She would make it. Forcing her feet to move faster, her knees to lift higher, she stepped up the pace. Soon she caught up with Vince, and her dad was right behind her. She wouldn't fall behind again.

"Thata girl. You can do it!" her dad encouraged her.

Now the trail got tougher, and Tess worked hard not to let her hopes and dreams fall onto the ground before her. The path grew steep and smooth from the feet of thousands of hikers. The park had built steps, laying large logs across the path and embedding them in the earth. These gave hikers a grip on the way down the hill. Tess's feet were almost straight up and down, her toes jammed into the rim of her new boots. But she kept up with Vince.

This is tough, but I am too. I will not fall behind. She began to jog. All of a sudden, the earth beneath her gave way. A large rock twisted out of the trail, twisting Tess's ankle with it.

"Oh no!" she cried out, as she slipped and fell. Her hip hit the ground so hard she thought she had landed on concrete.

"Tess, are you all right?" Her dad, only a few feet behind her, caught up with her quickly. Vince and the others had heard her fall and had turned around and come back to help. She looked up and tried to focus on the people around her. Her hip throbbed, and so did her ankle.

"I think, uh, think so," she said. Her dad helped her to her feet, and she dusted off her shorts.

"Walk around slowly for a minute. And take a drink," he said.

Tess walked in a small circle, happy that no one besides her dad had been directly behind her on the trail. How embarrassing, to fall in front of everyone. They were probably thinking they were going to have to baby her the whole way now. She would show them.

After a few minutes, her dad asked, "Are you ready to go?"

"Yes, " she said. "I feel much better." She tried not to be hurt when she saw her dad look at his watch.

"Okay then, that's the trouper!" Vince said. "Let's head off."

Only a little while longer, Tess told herself, and it was true. She tried not to think about how much her legs and feet hurt, instead counting the scruffy little cacti that speckled the trail on either side. They were round and furry, like the hairballs Erin's cat, Starlight, threw up.

Starlight had been a gift from Tess last November. *I gave Erin an orange cat; she gave me her orange hat.* Tess laughed. She didn't want to let her friend down. She would keep going. She knew she could do it. This was her big chance. And she didn't want the weekend to be a bust.

Within the hour, the team came to the Kaibab suspension bridge, which spanned the Colorado River. Just to the other side of that was Phantom Ranch and rest.

She stepped onto the shaky bridge, and it swayed a bit

beneath her feet. Tess looked at the other side, four hundred feet away, and at the river, nearly one hundred feet below her. The muddy Colorado River looked more like hot chocolate with whipped cream froth than the clear blue water she had expected. Tess saw Vince and the rest of the team on the other side, waiting, and she decided to hurry across. As she did, she felt something that struck fear into her heart.

She was hoping and praying that it was just the bridge. But deep inside, she knew why her right ankle—but not her left—felt shaky. That fall had damaged the already tender ankle.

nine

Phantom Ranch

Saturday, Just Before Noon, May 17

A few minutes after crossing the suspension bridge, they arrived at Phantom Ranch where they would spend the night. The ranch was an older building framed in weathered timbers. Tess noticed some well-tended mules grazing just outside the front door. Home never looked so good.

She heaved her pack off and set it on the ground. Stretching her arms, she bent over at the waist to stretch out her back, too.

"We made great time," Vince said, marking down the time on a small yellow pad he had brought along.

"I'll go check in for us, and you can wait here for the other teams, if you want," Tess's dad said to Vince, who agreed. Tess and her dad went to register.

Phantom Ranch sat among knobby little cacti and other scraggly plants near Bright Angel Creek. Long, black beams framed slightly dusty walls; huge rocks lined the outside walls. Tess peeked inside the dining room where a couple of people sat drinking iced tea. Then she joined her dad at check-in.

"Four of us share a room," her dad said, tucking the registration papers into the back pocket of his khaki shorts. "So, do you want the upper bunk or the lower bunk?" he teased.

"I'll take the lower bunk," Tess said, kidding. She knew her dad would rather be on the bottom, and she couldn't imagine him scrambling to the top.

"You did a great job today," her dad said, as they headed outside to retrieve their packs and to give Vince his set of room keys.

"Thanks, Dad," Tess said. "I feel pretty good about it. Except..." Her words trailed off.

"What?" Her dad stopped just shy of reaching the other team members. A concerned look crossed his face.

"Well, when I tripped, I think I twisted my ankle." She pointed to her feet. "The right one."

"Uh-oh," her dad said. "The one you twisted on Squaw Peak. Let's give the keys to the others, grab our gear, and I'll look at it in the room."

When they arrived at the room, Tess tossed her backpack onto the rough wooden dresser squeezed in at the foot of the bunk beds. Her backpack was covered with dust, as was everything else that had been on the trail with her. She sat down on the lower bunk and unlaced her boots.

"Let's see that," her dad said, peeling off one of her dirt-encrusted socks, soaked through with sweat.

He touched the puffy skin around the joint, and it left a slight indentation before slowly inflating again. "Hmm. This is a little swollen. Does it hurt?"

"Just a little," Tess admitted.

"Let's see the other foot," her dad said, peeling off the second sock.

"I don't like the look of that toenail," he said, examining her big toe. "It looks a little bruised underneath. How does it feel?"

"Kind of tender," Tess said.

"Well," her dad said, "I think I have just the cure for us. Let's put on our bathing suits, grab the sack lunches we brought from the lodge, and head to the river. I think some cool water will do those feet a world of good. I know it'll be good for me!"

"That sounds fun," Tess agreed, relieved that he didn't seem too worried about the ankle. That must mean things would turn out okay. She grabbed her bathing suit out of her pack and headed toward the bathroom.

Stripping the dirty clothes from her body, she stuffed them into the plastic bag her mom had tucked into her pack so the clean clothes wouldn't get dusty too. Tess put on her bathing suit and pulled a big T-shirt over the top, then slipped her feet into flip-flops. What a relief to have the whole day ahead for rest.

After she came back into the room, her dad went into the bathroom and changed too. When he came out, they grabbed their lunches.

"Want to play some chess down there?" he asked, picking up the mini-chessboard.

"Sure," Tess agreed. The two of them slung their towels over their shoulders and headed toward the creek. As they went out the front door, the second team from her dad's office was checking in. Dust creased their faces, and streams of sweat ran down their necks.

"Hey, did you take a nap on the trail or what?" Tess's dad teased.

"Aw, we're not that much later than you. And we're just

giving you a head start for tomorrow!" her dad's friend replied.

A few minutes later, after stepping in and around the grubby landscape, Tess and her dad found themselves at the bank of Bright Angel Creek. The bubbling stream was clear where the Colorado River had been murky. Tess could barely wait to wade in and cool off. Several other hikers were there too, but she and her dad found a great spot and put down their towels.

"Let's go in!" Tess waded in, and the cool water lapped against her swollen ankle and sore toenail, bringing immediate relief. "Ah, Dad, this is wonderful!" *Just what I need*, she thought. "This will really bring the swelling down. I'll be ready for tomorrow."

"Here I come!" Her dad ran into the water.

"Don't splash me!" she cried, as he dunked himself all the way under, then shook off like a dog, of all things.

"Dad!" Tess said. How could he? In front of everyone? But she couldn't help giggling.

They found some cool rocks to sit on, letting the water swirl around their ankles and calves before heading back to the soft cotton towels for their picnic lunch.

"I wonder what we have," her dad said. He unwrapped the top of his paper bag.

Tess unrolled hers too. "Turkey sandwich, baby bag of chips, apple, chocolate mints. And a Power Drink." She unscrewed the cap of the drink and took a long guzzle of the electric green liquid. "Ah." The liquid refreshment slid down her throat. She screwed the cap back on before taking the plastic wrap off her sandwich.

"Me, too," her dad said, drinking deeply. "This feels good,

and the lunch sounds wonderful." They ate, and her dad unfolded the traveling chessboard.

"It's fun to be here together," she said.

"It is," her dad agreed. They played one game, and no one seemed to have an obvious advantage. Then, "Checkmate!" Tess exclaimed.

"I think it's a sign," her dad said. He put the pieces into the holding space in the back of the board, folded it up, and stuck it into their pack.

"A sign of what?" Tess asked.

"That you'll win the hike, too," her dad said. He smiled, but Tess couldn't tell if he was teasing or felt he had to encourage her. "You can race ahead tomorrow right at the end and pull ahead of Vince, just like you won this chess game."

"Oh sure," Tess said. She reached down and touched her ankle. Although the water had made her ankle feel better, it was still puffy. Maybe just as puffy as it had been before.

"Maybe I should soak it in the water some more," she said.

"Good idea. Then, when we get back to the room, I'll wrap it in an Ace bandage for the evening. And we can put some antibacterial gel on that toenail, and a little Band-Aid, too. I'll bet they'll be all better in the morning."

"Yeah," Tess said. But a look passed between them as they walked back to the water. Tess wasn't at all sure that things would be better by morning, and from the look on her dad's face, he wasn't sure either.

ten

First Place

Saturday Night, May 17

Tess spent much of that afternoon napping and reading the magazine she had tossed into her backpack at the lodge. Her dad napped on the bunk below her. Just before dinnertime, she pulled Erin's pocket Bible out of her pack and scrambled back up to the top bunk to read it. As she let the words soften her heart, peace washed over her like rain on an untended garden.

It feels really good to read the Bible, Lord. I wonder why I always forget that and think spending time with you will be such a hassle. After a while she closed the Bible and tucked it under her pillow, closing her eyes one more time as a beefy scent coiled its way down the hall and snaked into the room.

"Smells like dinner. What do you say, cupcake?" her dad asked. She felt the bunk bed creak and sway as he sat up on the bunk beneath her.

"It does. And I am so hungry!" Tess said. She carefully climbed down the ladder, not wanting to twist her ankle by jumping. She slipped her flip-flops back on.

"How's the ankle?" her dad asked, unwrapping the bandage a little.

Tess held her breath. She didn't want to say anything to him about it. He wanted them to win so much.

"I think it's looking a little better. Not quite as swollen."

Before he wrapped it back up, Tess glanced down. To her, it looked just as swollen as it always had. And it still hurt. Just a little.

Tess's dad brushed his hair, looking into the small, warped mirror hanging on the wall. His whisker stubble cast a shadow over his face. It made him look angry. Tess pulled her hair back into a ponytail, and they headed toward the dining room.

"Where should we sit?" Tess asked. Vince and the others on their team were already seated, but no places were available by them.

"How about here?" Her dad pointed to a table occupied by a man and his teenage son. "This taken?" her dad asked.

"No, not at all. Sit down, Jim." The man indicated two places at their table. "This is my son, Jake. Jake, this is Jim Thomas."

"Nice to meet you," Jake said. He had a nice smile and thick, slicked-back black hair. Tess noticed he had a beaten silver ring on his middle finger with a black Christian fish on it. She smiled.

"And this is my daughter, Tess," Mr. Thomas said. "This is Alex Horton, and his son, Jake."

"Nice to meet you, too," Tess said.

They chatted for a few minutes while the waitress served iced tea with lemon wedges. Tess opened a packet of Sweet'n Low and stirred it in.

Another couple, a husband and wife named Ron and Patti, sat down at the table with them, and introductions were made.

"What did you order?" Tess asked the lady sitting next to her.

"Hiker's stew," she answered. "I'm so hungry it wouldn't matter what it was!"

"Me, too. I mean, I also ordered the hiker's stew. And I'm also so hungry I could care less!" Tess laughed. Soon enough her stew arrived, thick with beef, carrots, and tender pearl onions. The cornbread was warm and moist. Her dad and most of the others had ordered the steak, but it didn't look as good as her stew.

For a few minutes, no one talked; they just enjoyed the food. Then Jake broke in. "I see you're wearing cross earrings," he said to Tess. "Are you a Christian?"

Tess swallowed her mouthful and looked at her dad out of the corner of her eye. He looked straight ahead.

"Yes," she answered.

"Cool!" he said. "Me, too." Everyone took another bite and stayed silent.

"I didn't know you were a Christian, Jim," Mr. Horton said to Tess's dad.

Oh, Lord, help us out here, Tess prayed.

"I'm not," her dad answered. The second silence at the table seemed thicker than the first.

"Me neither," the woman next to Tess said. She still smiled and had a pleasant tone but added, "I always found it hard to understand how any kind of a god can let all the bad things happen that go on in this world. And especially how a father, a god, could send his own son to his death. As a parent, I could never do that. So that kind of takes care of Christianity for me." She forked in another mouthful of stew.

"That's kind of been my feelings too," Tess's dad said.

Tess didn't want to speak. *Please, let Jake say something. Or Mr. Horton.* But they didn't say anything. The pressure on her heart told her she had to say something. She searched for her most respectful voice. "Well, I haven't been a Christian all that long." Tess's mouth was dry, and sipping the tea didn't help. "But I guess what I've learned is that God gives us all choices in this world, and some of our bad decisions lead to bad things happening. That's not God's fault. He didn't make us like little robots. He gave us choices. And as for sending his son to die, well, the reason God made such a big sacrifice is that he loves us so much. He did something tough because he wants to be with us. So it was worth it. And he didn't make Jesus do that. Jesus went willingly."

The woman next to Tess said, "Well, yes," and then kept eating. Tess didn't dare look at anyone.

But soon afterward her dad stood up and said, "I'm finished. Are you ready to go back, Tess?"

Tess looked down at her half-finished stew. "I guess so."

Her dad looked at her bowl.

"Go ahead and finish your dinner. I'll wait for you outside." He strode from the room.

Tess looked at the faces around her. Jake smiled at her, but she didn't feel like smiling back. She finished her meal, the others around her chatting lightly about tomorrow's hike—which was mostly uphill—and the hot-air-balloon-ride prize for first place.

"We're not trying to win this year," Mr. Horton said.

"We're enjoying the view instead. We ran so fast last year we hardly saw anything! We decided at the last minute not to race but to come along with the company teams anyway."

The woman next to Tess laughed and started to tell a story about her hike last year. Tess nodded politely but, as soon as she could, excused herself.

Just as her dad had said, he was waiting right outside the dining room. He sat on a boulder watching the sunset.

Now I've done it, Lord, she prayed. *Not only have I twisted my ankle, but I've totally embarrassed my dad in front of all the people he works with. He's never going to want to go places with me again.*

But she didn't say any of this out loud. Instead, she asked, "Do you want to play another game of chess?"

"I don't think so," her dad answered. His voice wasn't mad. It wasn't sad. It was confusing. She couldn't quite figure it out.

"I think I'll read a little bit, and then we should get to sleep early. We have a long day ahead of us tomorrow." He half smiled. Tess exhaled. Maybe he wasn't too angry.

"Okay." They walked back to their room, and Tess went into the bathroom. She put on some lightweight sweats for sleeping and brushed her teeth. Then she returned to the room and climbed up to her bunk. After reading the comics section of a newspaper her dad had left on the table, she lay down. Vince and his friend weren't back yet, but they would climb into their own bunks whenever they were ready to sleep. Reaching her hand under her pillow, she felt the Bible she had tucked in there earlier.

Please help us to get first place, she prayed. *Dad really wants to win, and I want it to be a special time for us together.*

And then there's always the campfire tomorrow night. You didn't forget about that, did you, Lord? Tomorrow was going to be all uphill. Her toenail hurt a little. The ankle wasn't better, although it didn't really ache.

She felt a strange question well up inside. *Who's in first place in your life, Tess?*

You are, Lord, she answered back in her heart. A sweet peace wrapped around her, warmer than the downy cotton blanket she had pulled up to her neck, as her dad switched out the light. Tess drifted off to sleep, reassured. It must mean that they would win after all.

eleven

A Decision

Sunday at Sunrise, May 18

The next morning, Tess woke up before anyone else had stirred. She pulled her clothes out of the dust-encrusted pack and sneaked into the bathroom.

First, she tossed on a fresh T-shirt and some shorts. Next, she sat down on a cold chair in the bathroom to look at her ankle. It wasn't as swollen as it had been yesterday, but it still looked a little thick. After pulling on some fresh socks, she slipped into her hiking boots, grabbed the *Guide,* the canyon hiker's paper, and her Bible. Then she tiptoed out the door.

Her dad would be angry if she went too far away, so she perched on the same stone he had sat on last night, just outside the door. The morning chill was still thick in the air. She pulled her sweat jacket around her, as her breath sent out puffs of steam.

It was easy to pray in the silence, with the sun climbing up over the canyon walls. Mist hung in the air, almost like clouds kissing the ground. As the sun rose, it tinted the haze orange and scattered pink rays into the stony creases of earth.

Dear God, what should I do? Is my ankle healed? Do you want me to get well? I think you would. That way maybe Dad wouldn't be embarrassed, like he was last night at the dinner table. If we won, he wouldn't be embarrassed. And then there's that nasty Coronado Club business at the campfire tonight. Tonight! Is it that soon?

She opened the *Guide,* scanning the map sections for the day's hiking trails to the North Rim. As she flipped through the pages, a paragraph caught her eye.

"Every year, scores of unprepared hikers, lured by initially easy downhill hiking, experience severe illness, injury, or death from hiking in the inner canyon. Individuals creating a hazardous condition for themselves or others through unsafe hiking practices are subject to citation and/or arrest."

Citation and/or arrest? Is hiking on my ankle unsafe? Tess shifted on the rock, trying to find a comfortable position. Goose bumps ran up and down her legs. She did remember seeing someplace that it cost two thousand dollars if a helicopter had to take you out of the canyon.

She kept reading.

"Be prepared. Hike intelligently. You are responsible for your own safety."

She closed the paper and set it underneath her Bible so it wouldn't blow away.

Dear God, heal my ankle. Please. In Jesus' name, amen.

As the sun rose higher, warmth flooded through the valley and melted the mist. After her prayer, Tess's heart grew warmer too. She stood up, certain that God would heal her. She picked up her Bible and headed toward the room to meet her dad and the others.

"Up early, huh, kiddo?" Tess's dad was already dressed when she reached the room.

"Probably warming up so she can lead the pack today," Vince teased. "Well, I'm heading to the dining room. I'll meet you there."

"How's the ankle?" her dad asked. "Lemme look at it." Tess unwrapped her sock.

"Hmm," her dad said, poking it lightly. "Does this hurt?"

"No," Tess answered honestly. It did throb a little. But she didn't mention that.

"Good!" her dad seemed satisfied. "And the toenail?"

"I put a Band-Aid on it, but it really doesn't hurt at all today," Tess said.

"Good again. We're ready!"

Tess tucked the Bible into her shorts pocket and set down the *Guide* on the table in the room. "I'm starving!" she said. Then she and her dad walked to breakfast.

The room was noisy with the anxious buzzing of hikers, excited and jittery about the day ahead. The riding crowd sat together too. They would be heading back to the South Rim today on mules.

Platters of scrambled eggs, flapjacks, and crunchy bacon and tall glasses of juice appeared at each table. Everyone ate heartily. Tess looked around, then breathed a sigh of relief. Mr. Horton and Jake were at a table across the room, and she saw no sign of the woman who didn't want to be a Christian.

Her dad asked for a refill on his coffee and sat back,

looking content. "I think I'll get our sack lunches. We're supposed to start in about an hour so we can hike across before the hottest part of the day," he said. "Do you want to come with me?"

Tess reached into her pocket and felt her Bible. "No, I think I'll wait for you in the room."

Her dad nodded and walked off. She gulped the last of her orange juice and headed toward the room. She hadn't even made it all the way there when she felt a tiny throb in her ankle.

I'll wrap it, she thought. *That'll help. And it doesn't really hurt.*

After wrapping it in the Ace bandage, she climbed up on her bunk to read her Bible. She wanted to start right this morning, even if she wasn't in church on Sunday.

She let the Bible fall open. It opened to Proverbs 19. She read the first verse without much thought. The second verse, though, was different.

"Enthusiasm without knowledge is not good. If you act too quickly, you might make a mistake."

Am I making a mistake, being so enthusiastic about winning, but not "hiking intelligently," as the Guide *said?*

She closed her eyes and prayed. And waited for the answer. And when it came, tears welled up in her eyes. No matter what, though, she was going to finish reading this chapter. She had promised herself she would.

Her heart thumped when she reached verse 21. She whispered it aloud to herself. "People can make many different plans. But only the Lord's plan will happen."

She quickly skimmed the rest of the verses and snapped the Bible shut.

Why wouldn't hiking be God's plan? She had worked really hard and deserved to make it, deserved, in fact, to win.

But she knew in her heart she had heard her answer. God had told her in lots of ways. Through the tiny vibrations in her ankle. Through the strong words in the *Guide.* The quiet voice whispering to her heart. And through the Bible itself.

"But, God!" she wailed in the empty room.

"What was that all about?" her dad asked, as he stepped into the room with two sack lunches.

Startled, Tess didn't respond right away. But she knew if she was going to say anything, it was now or never. Never seemed like the better choice. But she started anyway. "Dad, can we talk for a minute?"

"Yeah." He sat down on his bunk. "Why don't you sit here with me?" He looked at his watch. "But hurry. We'll be leaving soon. Haven't you finished packing?"

Tess looked at her backpack, which oozed dirty clothes and some sunblock and had untied straps. "I'll do it in a minute," she said. She cleared her throat. She would give any amount of money for a glass of water. Or a way out of this.

Just then, Vince stepped into the room. "Hey, you two, we had better go. Only a couple of minutes till the teams take off, and we don't want to be late. Say, Jim, could you come outside for just a minute and help me with Danny's rigging? He has something going on with the backpack, and I need to check it out."

Not now, Vince, please, Tess thought.

"Sure," Tess's dad stood up. "Why don't you pack up

your gear and meet me outside? We can talk there." He patted Tess on the shoulder and left.

Great. It's bad enough to have to tell him, but now she had to make this huge announcement in front of everyone. She felt like a pimple on the face of the earth.

twelve

Shocked!

Sunday Morning, May 18

After her dad left the room, Tess gathered her belongings into the backpack. First, she shoved the dirty clothes bag to the bottom. The swimsuit was still damp, making the whole bag smell slightly moldy. Next, she stuffed in her magazine and the *Guide.* Finally, she put in her Bible, then pulled the string, and zipped it up. She looked around the room one last time before leaving. It seemed lonely now. Empty and let down.

As she walked outside, she noticed the sun was definitely in command. The mist had evaporated completely, and the rays were building up heat even at this early hour. Tess navigated around some of the other hikers and finally found her dad fixing the straps on Danny's pack.

"Here I am," she announced. "Looks like you have the pack all fixed up." She forced a smile into her voice, but it took too much work to keep it there. Sorrow crept in and made itself at home. She just couldn't do it. She couldn't say it. But she had to.

"Yep, it's all ready. Are you?" her dad asked. He pulled

his arm into the backpack strap and flung the pack over his shoulder, positioning it to walk. "We had better go meet Vince and the others."

"Uh, Dad, can we talk?" Beads of sweat burst out all over her scalp, although her hair hid them. One did trickle down her back.

"Yes, of course! I forgot you had something to tell me." Her dad looked at Danny, who was still standing nearby.

"Oh, yeah, right. Thanks for the help, Jim," he said before moving away. "I'll go find Vince."

Tess and her dad stood apart from the crowd.

"It's about my ankle," Tess said.

"Is it hurting again?"

"Well, not really. But it is still swollen, and it's throbbing a little bit. I prayed about it this morning, and I don't think I should race."

"What do you mean? Do you plan to stay here? Get a mule? Mom and Tyler are driving over to the North Rim today." He sounded angry.

"No, I can make it across. I think. I mean, I think I should take it easy. Walk slowly. But I'm sure I can make it." She didn't look him in the eye.

"Oh, Tess, I didn't think you would quit."

"Dad, I'm not quitting!" she said, looking up now. Tears threatened to break out. But they wouldn't have anywhere to hide, so she squeezed them back. "I read in the *Guide* about hiking smart. And running on my ankle, as much as you know I want to, isn't smart. I don't want to have a helicopter or a mule take me out!"

Mr. Thomas walked over to a nearby bench and sat down. He took off his pack. Tess sat next to him but not too close. Had she done the right thing or made a big mistake?

"Tess, you're right. You shouldn't race. I kind of thought that yesterday, but I didn't want to believe it. I wanted to believe we could win this thing together. You know? But you're wise. We can't do it that way."

Tess exhaled slowly, silently. He did understand. And now there was no question that she would make it. They would go slow, together. And she would get across, for sure.

"I'd better make some arrangements," her dad said. He patted her knee. "Wait here for me, okay?"

Her pack felt light on her shoulders now that she had told him the truth. Everything might turn out okay after all. They really hadn't seen much on the way down. Going more slowly would let them see all kinds of cool things. Like the Anasazi villages carved into the walls. Now that was something to look forward to! She hoped Vince wouldn't be too mad. Maybe if the team won without Tess and her dad, Vince would invite them to come along on the balloon ride anyway.

A few minutes later Tess saw her dad walking back across the compound toward her. Mr. Horton and his son, Jake, trailed behind him. They probably wanted to say good-bye. Tess hoped they wouldn't mention the little incident at dinner last night.

"Tess," her dad said, "do you remember Mr. Horton and Jake from dinner last night?"

Tess smiled. "Of course."

"Well," her dad continued, "I don't know if you remember their saying that they aren't trying to race. They're taking it easy, especially on the way up."

"I remember," Tess said. Maybe she and her dad would join the Hortons.

"I asked them if it would be okay for you to finish the hike with them today since you need to take it easy on the ankle. They've hiked this before, and they know the way and how to play it safe. I feel perfectly comfortable with your joining them."

Tess said nothing. Could she have heard wrong? Was he saying he was going without her? She looked at Mr. Horton, whose smile was about as strong as a cup of weak tea. Jake stared at his bootlaces. She realized they both understood how she felt. Abandoned by her own father. She didn't say a thing.

Tess remembered the verse she had heard last month in church. Josh Carrington got to pick the Bible chapter, and he had chosen the first chapter in Joshua because of his name. *I will never leave you alone.*

But no matter what God said, her father here on earth *was* leaving her alone. It was unbelievable.

"Tess?" Her dad looked at her. "Are you okay with that?"

"Yeah. I guess so." Even to herself her voice sounded flat.

"Good!" He kissed her cheek and strapped on his pack again. "I'm sorry you won't be able to be with us when we win, cupcake. But I'll wait for you at the top, and it'll work out best for everyone. I wouldn't want your ankle to be hurt before Outdoor School. Make sure you drink and refill your water. And don't forget to eat your sack lunch. They packed bagels."

"I will." Tess didn't look at him but past him, not trusting herself. She couldn't care less if the bagels ended up in the trash.

"I'll make sure she's okay," Mr. Horton said.

"Thanks again," Tess's dad said. Then he dashed off to

catch up with Vince. Tess looked up then and saw him from a distance, his red bandanna and hat easy to trail. Vince's group already was jogging up the path. She still couldn't believe she was being left behind.

The three of them stood around for a minute. Most of the others had left, and the mules were carefully plodding their way back to the South Rim.

Jake cleared his throat. "Well, we're cool with your coming with us and all. Sorry it didn't work out the way you wanted."

"It's okay," Tess said. It wasn't. Her ankle hurt much worse than it had just a few minutes before. What if she couldn't make it at all? She already was going to have to tell the whole sixth grade she didn't win first place. She just couldn't face them with the news that she had to be hauled out of the canyon on a mule. Why had she ever agreed to do this hike anyway?

"We had better get going, even if we're strolling." Mr. Horton tried to make his comment lighthearted. "It's still going to get hot even at a slower pace."

Tess tightened her pack. Mr. Horton strapped on his pack, and Tess caught a peek of the book he was reading. She had seen it at the bookstore. It was about the time just before Jesus came back to earth.

Jesus, this would be a good day to come back, she thought. Her heart felt as heavy as a sack of the sandy soil that lay between her and the North Rim.

thirteen

One Step

Sunday, May 18

"It's nearly fourteen miles to the top," Jake said.

"I hadn't realized that." Fourteen miles! It was only ten down, and that had seemed like a lot. And it had been downhill. Tess became more and more convinced she wasn't going to make it at all. Would a ranger be available to come and haul her out?

"You know what they say?" Mr. Horton said.

"What's that?" Tess asked. She tried to be polite. She knew Mr. Horton and Jake were trying too. After all, Jake probably wasn't too excited about a twelve-year-old girl tagging along with him and his dad.

"The journey of a thousand miles—or, in our case, fourteen miles—begins with a single step."

A thousand miles. That's just what this feels like to me.

Prickly pear cactus clung to the sides of the trail, hiding dying blossoms behind fleshy, hand-shaped stems like shy Japanese ladies. Normally Tess would have noted the different shades of purple and green so she could tell her mom later. But now she kept her eyes trained on the powdery path ahead of her, willing herself to keep putting one foot in front of the other and not to trip on anything. At least her ankle was okay.

"Where do you go to church?" Jake asked.

"Living Water Community Church."

"Oh, hey, I've heard that's cool. I have some friends in its high school group."

"Where do you go to church?"

"Pleasant Valley. I play guitar there. I want to have a music ministry when I'm out of school. I mean, a couple of my friends and I are already playing some gigs. So we're getting ready, you know?"

"Dreams are always good," his dad offered, smiling as he said it. Tess noticed that he glanced at her right ankle. He really was keeping an eye on her, as he had promised her dad.

"Yeah. This trip was kind of a dream for me," Tess said. "And winning is a dream for my dad. I guess he'll get his dream." Tess sighed but didn't say anything after that. She unwrapped her red bandanna from her neck. It didn't match her orange hat at all, but it matched her dad's bandanna. Her mom had bought them matching ones and a red hat for her dad.

She wiped her forehead with the bandanna and took a long gulp of water. Then the three of them walked on. She had to make the best of this, or she wasn't going to get out of the canyon. She said she had put God in first place in her life, and now she had to trust that when he told her to do something, it was the right thing to do. And she was certain she was obeying him.

As the miles passed, Tess giggled at a couple of Jake's

jokes. Any other time, she would have been rolling with laughter. Wouldn't Tyler love him?

Tyler. Oh yeah. And Mom and Erin and the whole Janssen family would be waiting for her on the other side. And who would show up? Dad. How could she face them? Her cheeks were on fire with embarrassment and the heat of the day.

Fire. Oh yeah again. As in campfire tonight.

"Do you want to stop for lunch?" Mr. Horton asked.

"Sure." It had been a couple of hours, and Tess figured they were maybe halfway there. She took the *Guide* from her pack. Yep, halfway.

"Not bad for camping food, huh?" Jake took out his bagel sandwich, fruit, and sports drink. "Want some jerky?"

"Sure," Tess answered. She hoped it didn't get stuck in her teeth. *No more humiliating things today, please.* They rested in the shade of a twiggy tree. Its branches were gnarled and snarled, like big hair on a windy day. But it gave great shade, and some smooth rocks underneath it provided a place to sit.

They finished lunch and packed up. It was hot, and she was lonely. She had only one thing to look forward to, the Anasazi ruins. She had learned about them in school. These were the old homes of different tribes of native Americans who had lived in the canyon. It was amazing! They actually built their houses in these steep walls and climbed on sure feet to get into them. She had been in too much of a hurry to look for any of the dwellings on the way down, even though her dad was part native American.

"Hey, do you know anything about the Anasazi ruins?" she asked Mr. Horton. He had been this way before, after all.

"Not much. I know they're thousands of years old and that several different tribes made—and still make—their homes here. If you look carefully in the walls at different places, you can see the little window holes." Mr. Horton caught up with Tess. "Do you want to borrow my binoculars?"

"Sure," Tess said. Dad had taken theirs in his pack. She stopped and took them from Mr. Horton. They were lightweight but powerful. "Wow! You can really see far with these."

"They come in pretty handy at a football game," he joked.

She scanned the horizon and thought she saw the telltale signs of an Anasazi ruin in the peach-colored rocks, which were washed smooth but had a little window that looked out on the world. She could almost imagine a girl like her living there.

"Would you like to keep them for a while?" Mr. Horton nodded at the binoculars.

"Okay, thanks." Maybe it would pass the time. It would take her mind off how tired she was, that her ankle was starting to hurt, and that her toenail was biting into her skin. That her dad wasn't with her, even though they had been practicing together for nine months.

As Tess hiked, she became more tired with each step. Nothing around her looked new, and most of the other teams had passed them. It was empty on this stretch.

"I think I'll look for a minute," she said, using the binoculars as an excuse to rest. She scanned the trail ahead of her. It was going to become even steeper soon, she knew. Far ahead she saw something. A cactus flower? No. A red hat. And a bandanna. It must be her dad, although she couldn't see his face. And now she saw the sturdy figure of Vince and the others. They were into some switchbacks. *Oh, Dad, I wish we were together.*

She set the binoculars back around her neck and kept hiking, chatting with Jake and Mr. Horton to pass the time. She didn't want them to think she was snotty or anything. It was nice of them to let her come along. And besides, she might really need to rely on them to get her up the hill. Fear crawled up her spine. Would she have to lean on them all the way up—if she made it at all?

She stopped again, pretending she just wanted to use the binoculars again. She scanned the trail ahead and frowned.

"I wonder where my dad is."

"What?" Jake asked.

"A little while ago I saw my dad on the trail ahead. Now I don't see him at all." She scanned the scrub oak ahead of them. Dad must be behind a tree or something.

"Maybe they're behind a switchback. I wouldn't worry."

"Naw, I won't." She scanned the horizon again. But she did worry. Where was he?

"Wait! I see them. And…and he's sitting down. My dad is on a rock, and Vince and Danny are standing right next to him. They're looking at my dad!"

"Maybe they're just drinking some water," Jake suggested.

"Nobody's drinking," Tess said. "Besides, the rest of the group is moving forward up the trail. I can see them." What if her dad was hurt and they were trying to figure out what to do?

She didn't want to say anything about that possibility, but Mr. Horton took the binoculars from her.

He looked at the trail ahead. "You're right, Tess. I think there's some kind of difficulty."

"Don't worry, kid. There's nothing we can do," Jake said. "Let's pray about it and move forward. Maybe we'll catch up with him. The journey of fourteen miles is one step after another, remember."

Yeah, but your dad isn't hurt or in trouble, Tess thought. *And mine is.*

fourteen

Ribbon Falls

Sunday, May 18

Tess needed to catch up with her dad. She walked faster, moving ahead of Mr. Horton and Jake.

"Am I going too fast?" she asked.

"No, it's cool," Jake said. She thought that was pretty nice. She knew they didn't want to hurry. But now things were different. She didn't even waste time checking the binoculars, not wanting any delay.

In less than an hour she had reached Ribbon Falls, where a pale blue stream of water soothed layers of sandstone and granite blanketed with emerald moss. Just around a switch-back, Tess spied her dad walking toward her as fast as she was toward him. He was coming back to her! She started to jog but noticed that Mr. Horton and Jake were slowing down, allowing her and her dad time to be together alone.

"Dad!" Tess ran to meet him, in spite of the sharp spearing pain from her toenail and the tender throbbing of her ankle.

He smiled, jogging toward her. The two of them sat down in a little shade patch near the water.

"Are you thirsty?" he asked.

"Yes." Tess took a drink of her water and looked at her dad. "Where's Vince? Why were you walking back toward us?" She looked at her watch. "You'd better hurry. Another one of the teams from work passed us a few minutes ago. You must have seen them!"

Tess's dad's face looked as though it was in pain as he saw her look at her watch.

"I'm not trying to win, cupcake."

"But, Dad, why not? Mr. Horton loaned me his binoculars, and I saw you on the trail. You guys were way ahead of everyone else. You could have made it!"

"I saw you on the trail too, Tess. Before you looked at me. I could see your neon orange hat." He tapped the rim of her hat, which now was peach-colored from the dust rather than orange. His face both glowed with love and was lined with sorrow.

"When I saw you, my heart was breaking. I watched you picking your way through the trail and the rocks, being so brave. Trying so hard. And alone."

Tess tried not to spill the tears. "I had the Hortons," she said. Now that he was back, she loosened the sorrow she had tightly bound up in her heart. Her dad saw and put his arm around her.

"Yes, but you needed your father to be with you, and I realized I wanted to be with you more than anything. More than winning. No matter what sacrifice I had to make, we needed to be together. And now we are." He looked at her. "I guess I made one of those bad decisions you were talking about last night. Will you forgive me?"

"Yes, Dad, of course." She snuggled in closer.

He held her, and she melted into his arms. Her daddy

was back. The falls giggled behind her, and all was well in her life, for this moment, at least.

"But what about the balloon ride—" she started.

Her dad interrupted her.

"Let me tell you something," he said. "But first, I'm going to send those two on their way."

He let go of her and went to talk with Jake and his dad. "Thanks for taking care of her." Her dad shook hands with both of them. "I think we can go it alone together from here. Father-daughter time and all that. I bet you two would appreciate some time alone too."

"She was no trouble at all, Jim. We enjoyed talking with her these past few hours," Mr. Horton said. "But I certainly understand. See you on the North Rim!"

They took off, and Tess's dad walked back to where she sat.

"I left the dinner table last night for two reasons," her dad explained. "One, I was kind of embarrassed to be talking about religion, as you probably guessed."

"I'm sorry about that," Tess said, wanting to say more.

But her dad said, "No, let me continue." He wiped his forehead with the dusty bandanna, leaving a smudge where the sweat used to be. "But also, it bothered me. I had never quite thought about what you said in that way. That maybe Jesus came willingly, to pay a price to be with us. For the first time, the message started to make sense to me and to touch me. But I didn't want it to. So I left."

Tess's heart trembled inside, but she kept quiet. If he saw her shaky hands he would think she was tired and not realize she was excited about what he was saying.

"Then today, when I was jogging ahead, and I looked back and saw you, my heart broke. I wanted so much just to be with you. I heard a voice inside say, 'Isn't that just what Tess was saying about God last night? He did what he had to do to be with his children. No matter what the cost.' And suddenly, it all clicked into place."

He held her close again, and she breathed deeply.

A minute or two later, Tess broke the silence. "This is so great. Does this mean you want to become a Christian?"

He shook his head no. Her heart fell.

"I mean, I don't know. I'm ready to investigate, to talk with some people. Maybe Erin's dad."

Tess smiled inside and out. "That's terrific," she said. "I'm so happy, Daddy. This is the best thing ever." Well, almost the best. The best would be having her dad say he wanted to be a Christian.

Then Jake's words came back to her. A journey begins with one step in the right direction. Her dad had turned around, and he was walking in the right direction. *Oh, Jesus, let him get there soon.*

"So how's the ankle?" her dad asked.

"It hurts a little," Tess admitted. "But the toenail hurts worse."

He checked out the swelling and wrapped it with another bandage, strengthening it. And then she took off her other hiking boot.

"Hmm, not good at all," her dad said. "The base of the toenail is black, bleeding underneath, I think. Must be the new boots."

He applied some antibacterial ointment and a bandage, and then she slipped on a fresh pair of socks that her dad fished out of her backpack.

"We had better get going. We have a whole slew of people waiting for us up top," her dad said.

"What if I don't make it?" Tess asked. "What if it gets too bad for me to keep going?"

"I'll carry you back," he said. A slow peace spread throughout her body. At that moment, she knew she could make it.

They walked the last—and toughest—five miles together. Tess barely noticed the pain in her ankle, watching tufts of cotton hitchhike on a breeze as they passed Cottonwood Campground.

Soon her dad said, "We're almost there. It's Uncle Jim Point!"

"Uncle Jim, ha-ha. Maybe they knew you would be passing by!" Tess said.

Then, on the long way up the rim, she began to think about the night that lay ahead of her. The wonderful news to tell Erin about her dad, the confusion her mother would have when she found out the same news. And, of course, telling the whole sixth grade that she had made it across, although not winning first place.

Will you tell them about your dad and your faith? a voice inside asked.

Uh-oh. Tess hadn't thought about that. Sharing her belief at a dinner table with a handful of strangers was a lot different from telling everyone in the sixth grade. Especially when she knew what Lauren and Colleen would have to say.

fifteen

North Rim

Sunday Afternoon, May 18

Tess was amazed when, just a few hours later, they made it to the top. The trek had been hot, sweaty, and sometimes painful, but she and her dad had made it together.

"I think we're in last place," Tess said to her dad, as they rounded the last few thousand feet.

"I think so too," he said. Then he smiled. "But that's okay, right?"

"Right," Tess said. And it was.

She heard a familiar shout from the top.

"It's Tess and Dad!" Tyler shouted. "By George, they made it after all." He started to run down the trail to meet them.

"I say, the old dear was getting a little worried about you two!" He caught up with his dad and gave him a hug.

"Want me to take your backpack?" Tyler asked Tess.

"Yes!" She gratefully shrugged off the straps and handed the pack over to her brother. They rounded the top together, and saw Erin and their mom sitting at a viewpoint.

"Mom!" Tess called out. She walked as fast as she could,

spending the last bit of energy in her legs to get to her mother. Then she burst into tears.

Her mother hugged her. “Are you all right, honey?” She looked at Tess’s father, who said nothing. “We talked to Vince a bit when he arrived without you. But what’s the story?”

“We didn’t win!” Tess blurted out.

“I know. It’s okay. You did a great job. I am totally in awe of you!” Erin reassured her, handing a bottle of sports drink to her Secret Sister. “I thought you might be thirsty. Want some?”

Tess took the bottle and drank it dry. “That was great, thanks.”

“We have a late checkout at the room. We came up last night,” Mrs. Thomas said.

“Last night? I thought you were coming today.” Tess’s dad’s eyebrows raised in surprise.

“Well, Josh got really sick, and the Janssens went home. They left Erin with us, and we decided to come over last night to spend some time here. Besides, we thought you guys could use a shower before getting in the car!” She hugged her husband. “But I want to know, are you okay? We saw Vince at least an hour ago, probably more. He said that something had happened to Tess and you had gone back for her. Where had you left her?”

“That’s a story for after the shower,” Mr. Thomas said. “We’re all okay. Let’s clean up and then meet for an early dinner before driving the girls to Outdoor School. If we don’t leave soon, we won’t get them there in time for the campfire.”

Erin looked at Tess. Tess dropped her head. Maybe missing the campfire wouldn't be such a bad thing. If they made it, she would have to face Lauren's rude comments about being a loser. And what about sharing her faith?

They went into the lodge, and Tess took the first shower. Then she and Erin went to the coffee shop to order Cokes and wait for the others.

"What happened?" Erin asked. "I mean, if you want to talk about it. Was it your ankle?"

Tess was still so thirsty. She drank her Coke and both her and Erin's water.

"Yes. The ankle *and* the toenail."

"What's up with the toenail?"

"I hurt it walking in new boots. And my dad says it's going to come off."

"Ooh, gross. So tell me all about it."

Tess filled her Secret Sister in on all the details about the hike down, including twisting her ankle. When she reached the part about dinner at Phantom Ranch, she told Erin, "So at dinner, this lady was kind of dissing Christianity. I spoke up and said something about it."

"No way!" Erin set down her Coke and looked around her before asking the next question. "What did your dad do?"

"He left the room."

"Oh, Tess, how awful. Did he get really mad? But he didn't look mad at you today."

Tess sipped her Coke and set it down. "I haven't told you the best part yet." She leaned across the table so she wouldn't have to talk too loudly. "This morning was so bad. I told my dad about my ankle bothering me, and he left me with this other guy and his son so he could still be on the winning team."

"Oh, that's bad. You must have felt terrible. Were your feelings hurt?"

Tess nodded, but a slow smile spread across her face. "But it turned out really great. Dad changed his mind and met me halfway. He said that he wanted us to be together, and after what I said last night, he was really interested in learning more about Jesus!" Now she was grinning.

"Oh, that is so great. I mean, who cares about winning?" Erin said.

"Exactly," Tess answered. "He said he might talk to your dad about it. So I was kind of bummed when I found out your parents went back home."

"Yeah, but they can talk next week when they come to pick us up at Outdoor School. Maybe I could call my mom and ask if just the dads could drive up."

"That's a great idea," Tess said.

"What do you think your mom is going to say about your dad since she's not a Christian either?"

"I don't know," Tess admitted. "But I have another problem I have to figure out before that."

"What?"

"The campfire."

"That shouldn't be such a big deal. I mean, I know you didn't win first place, and Lauren will pick on that, but you did make it across."

"But I have to tell my story in front of everyone."

"So? You probably saw lots of cool things. It'll be interesting."

Tess's family walked into the coffee shop just then. She nodded her head toward her dad. "I know. But just how much do I say about him? I mean, about my obeying God and not racing, and about my dad turning back and understanding about Jesus and all that. It makes sense to me. But you have to know the whole story, or it doesn't."

Erin understood. Sharing your faith in public was totally hard. "I see," she said. "Yeah, that's going to be a tough decision."

"Hi, girls!" Tess's mother slid in next to Tess. "I can barely squeeze this tummy into a booth anymore!"

"I think we'll sit on this side," Tyler said. "Say, old girl, fancy my new junior-ranger badge?"

He handed a patch over to Tess, who looked at it. She was about to crack a joke, but she saw the earnest look on his face. He wanted her to like it.

"This is really cool, Tyler," she said. "Did you have to do a lot of things to earn it?"

"Of course," he said. "But I did them all and went to the information station before we left the South Rim and got it! I'm going to have Mom sew it on my backpack."

"Since when does your mother sew?" Tess's dad joked.

The waitress arrived, and each ordered dinner and ate heartily. Tess tried to be ladylike and not gobble her food, but dinner had never tasted so good now that the hike was over. Besides, she reminded herself, she would need all her strength for tonight.

"We had better hit the road," her dad said. "We have a couple of hours of driving ahead of us, and we want to make it to Outdoor School on time. Then we three have to drive home."

"I'll drive," Mrs. Thomas said. "I know how tired you are." Erin looked at Tess, who winked but said nothing. Mrs. Thomas was not the best driver, and it made them all nervous at times.

"No, I don't mind," Tess's dad said. "I'll let you know if I get too tired."

Tess smiled at Erin and scooted out of the booth.

"Well, let's go!" Tess said. She would have two hours on the road to think about what she was going to say—or not say—tonight.

sixteen

Outdoor School

Sunday Evening, May 18

A few hours later they pulled into the campgrounds where Coronado Elementary held its annual Outdoor School for sixth graders.

"I wonder if Joann and Katie are here yet," Tess said as they drove into the large entrance. A big log cabin stood in front, with a spotlight highlighting a giant American flag that flapped in the breeze.

"They must be. Look at how many people are here!" Erin answered. Tons of kids milled about, some shouting in the volleyball pit, others walking their suitcases into the long rows of bunkhouses to the sides of the driveways. The wind rustled through the piney treetops, like giant Christmas trees telling secrets. The sun was nearly set; only tiny points of light filtered through into the camp itself.

"I think everyone is already here. I mean, it's pretty late," Tess said.

Mr. Thomas pulled the car into the graveled circle drive and shut off the engine. "Let's go to the office and see if the school has someone there to check you in," he said. Tyler and Mrs. Thomas got out of the car too.

"Tess! Erin! You're here! How did it go?" Katie came running over from the shuffleboard area. Joann handed her shuffleboard stick to someone else and came right behind her.

"It went great," Erin said.

Tess looked around her, but she didn't see anyone from the Coronado Club. They must be setting up the campfire.

"Let's check in, and we'll meet you at the cabin," Tess said. She followed her dad into the office and waited while he made sure that their counselor and teachers were all there. Then they walked outside.

"I guess we had better get going, cupcake," he said. "We still have another couple of hours to drive to get home. I think I'll even let Mom drive." His eyes twinkled.

"Dad, before you go, can I talk with you in private?" Tess asked. She saw the questioning look on her mother's face. But Tess wanted her father to make a promise before he had a chance to talk too much with her mom about Christianity.

"Okay." They walked a few feet to a triangle of pine trees.

"Well, you know how you said you would talk with Erin's dad? You haven't changed your mind, have you?"

"No, I haven't changed my mind," he said.

"Erin had a great idea. She thought maybe you and her dad could come up together, alone, to get us. Would that work?" *Please, Lord, let him say yes.*

"We'll see, honey, we'll see."

"But will you at least call her dad and ask him?"

"I'll call him. I promise." He kissed her cheek, and they walked back to the car together. "Be sure to change the bandage on that ankle each day. And keep putting ointment on that toenail. I talked with the nurse about it in the office."

Oh boy. Tess hoped the people who ran the camp didn't think she was an invalid or something.

"I will." Tess kissed her mother good-bye and gave Tyler a high-five before heading toward the cabin with Katie, Joann, and Erin.

Cabin number one was all that they had been promised. Knotty-pine walls gave the place a warm glow. It smelled slightly of campfire smoke and sap. A twin bed with a roll-away cot underneath it was for the counselor who would sleep in their room. Red-and-white-checked curtains covered the three windows, a tiny refrigerator stood in the corner, and two bunk beds waited for the girls. A tiny bathroom completed the cabin.

"None of the other cabins has a refrigerator," Katie pointed out proudly. "And we're the only one with four people. All the other rooms have eight or ten people in them. So we're private!"

Joann giggled. "We took the bunks over there, and we thought you guys would want the ones here." She pointed to the beds on the right. Katie already had her stuffed animal on her bunk. She didn't care if anyone thought it was cool or not. Tess smiled.

"Want the upper or the lower?" Erin asked her.

"Lower," Tess said. "I had the upper last night, thanks. And I don't feel like climbing anything right now." She tossed her suitcase onto the dresser, opened it, and stuffed all her clothes into one of the empty drawers. Erin unsnapped her suitcase too, but stacked her things neatly.

"Hi, girls!" A teenager, maybe seventeen years old, came

into the cabin. "My name is Deena. I'm your chaperone." She took the scrunchie out of her hair, then put it back in, pulling her ponytail even tighter. All four girls stared at her. She was gorgeous. How cool to be in high school.

"I'll be bunking here," she patted the twin bed. "And I'm here to help you with whatever you need, so don't be afraid to ask." She opened a can of iced tea. "We had better get going. The campfire is sure to start any minute, and we don't want to miss that. Hey, isn't one of you Tess?"

"Yes, me," Tess squeaked out.

"Cool! I guess you're talking about your hike, huh? Where's your blue ribbon?" She looked around the room, like maybe Tess had tossed it over a bedpost or something.

"Uh, I don't have one," Tess answered.

"Oh. I see. Well, don't worry about it. Just tell everyone about your hike. It'll be great. Besides, I think they have a skit and some marshmallows and stuff. So you only need to talk for a few minutes. See you there!" Then Deena left the room.

"Uh-oh. No blue ribbon, Tess?" Joann asked. "Lauren has been telling people all day that you weren't going to win, that you weren't going to make it across. That you weren't even going to show up tonight."

"Well, I'm here, aren't I?" Tess asked, pulling her arms into her sweatshirt. "I made it across, didn't I? So I guess Lauren doesn't know everything after all."

"But what are you going to tell them?" Katie asked.

seventeen

Campfire Tales

Sunday Night, May 18

"I really don't know what I'll say," Tess answered Katie. Pulling off her hiking boots, Tess put on her tennis shoes. "I guess I'll just tell everyone all about the hike. I'll just tell the truth." She looked at Erin, and Erin looked back at her. Tess felt acid rise in her throat.

"We'll meet you over there," Joann said. She and Katie opened the screen door and slammed it behind them.

"You know what just came to my mind?" Tess asked.

"What?"

"Well, last month I got grounded because I lied to my parents, so I never had the chance to share my testimony at Spring Fling. But maybe this is my chance to say something, even if it's something small."

"You're right. But that's kind of scary. I know when I was first telling you about Jesus, I was so afraid that you would think I was stupid and that you wouldn't want to be friends with me," Erin said. "I don't know if I would have been brave enough to do it in front of everybody."

"I don't know if I'm brave enough either," Tess admitted.

"But what if you hadn't shared with me? Come on, let's go."

The two of them walked along the footpath that led to the campfire site. The night was cool and vibrating with the chattering of nearly one hundred voices.

But the two Secret Sisters didn't add their voices to the clamor. Tess was too nervous, and Erin must have understood because she didn't say anything either. Finally they arrived at the campfire. A circle of river rock stretched at least ten feet across, and a huge stack of kindling, lightwood, and pine was piled inside, shaped like a tepee. Melody, from the Coronado Club, was helping Mr. Basil light the fire.

"There's the Coronado Club," Erin whispered.

Tess felt a little tug of fear. "I know. Lauren saw me and then whispered something to Colleen."

"Yeah. But Colleen walked away. Weird." The two of them sat down next to Katie and Joann, who had saved places for them on a fallen log.

Colleen came over to them. "Hi, guys. I think the skits are first, then you're going to talk, Tess. Did you bring your ribbon?"

"I don't have a ribbon," Tess said. "We came in last place."

"Oh." Colleen looked disappointed. Strange, Tess would have thought Colleen would have been happy she had failed.

"Do you still want to get up there?" Colleen asked. "You could back out, you know. Lauren's already told everyone you probably would back out."

"She's not backing out," Joann said coldly.

"Okay," Colleen said. "Right after the skit."

Tess heard a rustling noise from the bushes behind her

and was startled when what looked like a pirate jumped out of the dark trees behind them. Then she realized it was Mrs. Rodriguez, Tess and Erin's sixth-grade teacher.

"Hey, there! Give me your gold for a good cause!" Mrs. Rodriguez said. The girls giggled. Mrs. Rodriguez had on a green triangular hat with a red feather glued on it, and a pea green jacket.

"Robin Hood!" Katie said. "Oh, I wish we could have done the skit."

"Who's Maid Marian?" Erin asked.

"Lauren, I'll bet," Katie said. Mrs. Rodriguez pursed her lips to keep from laughing but nodded her head to indicate they were right.

"And look who they made be Little John," Tess said. "Colleen." She stared across the fire at Colleen's silly costume and sad face. But then the skit was about to start, and they all joined in the laughter as Mrs. Rodriguez helped "rob" Mr. Basil of all the loot in his bags.

After the skit was over, the loot bags were opened. Plastic bags of marshmallows fell out of one and chocolate squares out of another. Melody came around with wooden platters of graham crackers.

The fire snapped and crackled like supercharged Rice Krispies. When the voices died down, Lauren beckoned Tess forward.

"Now or never, I guess." Tess pulled her sweat jacket tightly around her. Erin started to join her, but Tess shook her head no. She would do this by herself.

Lauren leapt right in, making sure, as always, that she was the center of attention. "This is Tess Thomas, as a few of you probably know. She was supposed to hike the Grand Canyon this weekend and come in first place. From what

I hear, things didn't go quite as well as she had hoped." Lauren grinned. Her lopsided anti-smile pierced through the night to make Tess even colder.

"But in spite of it, she's agreed to put on a brave face and tell us about it."

A few people clapped as Tess walked over to the campfire.

"Well, my dad's company has teams of people who hike the Grand Canyon each year, and this year my dad and I decided to do it too."

She recounted the steep trails, the sweaty hours, the many quarts of water trying to dampen her dusty throat. She told all about the dining room and bubbling Bright Angel Creek.

"Why didn't you win if things went so well?" Jared Miching asked.

"I twisted my ankle on a loose stone. It was kind of a weak ankle, anyway, because I'd injured it hiking earlier this year. So then it kept swelling. I really wanted to win. But I was afraid I'd hurt it worse and a helicopter would have to get me out of the park."

"Cool! A helicopter ride would be awesome," someone shouted. A bunch of boys agreed.

"Yeah, if you have two thousand dollars, maybe," Tess said.

"Two grand! No way." The murmuring died down.

"So, do you feel like a loser, since you came in last place?" a girl's voice called out. It was dark beyond the fire, so Tess couldn't see who had asked that. But it sure sounded like Coronado Club member Melody Shirowsky.

Tess heard other voices in the crowd. She hadn't told

anyone where she had placed in the race except for Colleen and Erin. Colleen must have told the rest of the Coronado Club. She still couldn't keep quiet about the littlest thing, could she?

"Last place, that's bad," some people muttered.

"No, I don't feel like a loser." She took a deep breath and let the words rush forward on their own. She had never told a crowd of kids about her faith before.

"I'm a Christian, and my family isn't. But on this hike, for the first time, my dad said he was starting to understand what it meant to be a Christian. If I hadn't been hurt, he wouldn't have 'got it' at all. And to me, that was worth more than first place." She noticed a smile on the face of a boy she didn't know, sitting across the fire from her. She smiled back.

The circle was quiet for a minute, really quiet. Inside, Tess felt the quiet reassurance of God's approval. It was the only approval she needed.

Then a couple of people asked her some questions about the hike. A few minutes later she was through. She had done it!

Tess watched as Lauren whispered in Melody's ear and pointed at Tess. The two of them laughed at her as she made her way back to her seat. But no one else was laughing. Most people smiled at her.

"Very brave," Erin whispered to her. She handed her Secret Sister a licorice friendship knot and moved closer to her.

It was comfortable, Tess thought, to be with people who loved you.

"Well, it's not like I told them the whole gospel or anything," Tess said. She accepted the licorice and smiled at her friend. "But I did take one step in the right direction."

She looked out into the quiet edge of night. And deep inside, Tess knew that what she had done was exactly what she was supposed to do.

Have More Fun!!

Visit the official website at:
www.secretsisters.com

There are lots of activities, exciting contests, and a chance for YOU to tell me what you'd like to see in future Secret Sisters books! AND—be the first to know when the next Secret Sisters book will be at your bookstore by signing up for the instant e-mail update list. See you there today!

If you don't have access to the Internet, please write to me at:

Sandra Byrd
P.O. Box 2115
Gresham, OR 97030

Would you like to own your own Secret Sisters charms? You can buy a set that includes each of the eight silver charms Tess and Erin own—a heart, ponies, star, angel, Bible, paintbrush, dolphin, and flower bouquet. Please send $8 (includes shipping and handling) to: Parables Charms, P.O. Box 2115, Gresham, OR 97030. Quantities are limited.

Tumbleweeds

Want to make an authentic Arizona treat? Mix up a batch of delicious Tumbleweeds!

You'll need:

1 can (12 ounces) salted peanuts
1 can (7 ounces) potato sticks
3 cups butterscotch chips
3 tablespoons peanut butter

Combine peanuts and potato sticks in a bowl and set aside. Pour butterscotch chips and peanut butter in a glass bowl. Place butterscotch and peanut butter mixture in the microwave. Heat at 70% power for 1 to 2 minutes or until melted, **but be sure to stir every 30 seconds.** Add to peanut–potato stick mixture and stir together. Drop by heaping tablespoonfuls onto waxed paper and refrigerate until set, about 5 minutes.

You'll get the point, though I don't know when,
If you solve the riddle of what's in Book Ten!

Across

2 Riding path

4 Sleepover or Day, they're both fun in the summer.

7 Another word for "evening"

8 Tess's ex-best friend

9 The name of the ranch

10 Taking care of your horse

13 Where you go after elementary school

Down

1 Crawl-stroking

3 The kind of friends Tess and Erin are

5 The top prize

6 Where horses are kept

11 City where the camp is located

12 When you have a disagreement with someone, at times it's called a _____.

14 What the Secret Sisters like to ride

Answers: Across: 2Trail 4Camp 7Twilight 8Colleen 9Lazy K 10Grooming 13Junior high
Down: 1Swimming 3Best 5Blue ribbon 6Stable 11Tucson 12Fight 14Horses

Look for the other titles in
Sandra Byrd's Secret Sisters Series!
Available at your local Christian bookstore

Available Now:

#1 *Heart to Heart:* When the exclusive Coronado Club invites Tess Thomas to join, she thinks she'll do anything to belong—until she finds out just how much is required.

#2 *Twenty-One Ponies:* There are plenty of surprises—and problems—in store for Tess. But a native-American tale teaches her just how much God loves her.

#3 *Star Light:* Tess's mother becomes seriously ill, and Tess's new faith is tested. Can she trust God with the big things as well as the small?

#4 *Accidental Angel:* Tess and Erin have great plans for their craft-fair earnings. But after their first big fight will they still want to spend it together? And how does Tess become the "accidental" angel?

#5 *Double Dare:* A game of "truth or dare" leaves Tess feeling like she doesn't measure up. Will making the gymnastics team prove she can excel?

#6 *War Paint:* Tess must choose between running for Miss Coronado and entering the school mural-painting contest with Erin. There are big opportunities—and a big blowout with the Coronado Club.

#7 *Holiday Hero:* This could be the best Spring Break ever—or the worst. Tess's brother, Tyler, is saved from disaster, but can the sisters rescue themselves from even bigger problems?

#8 *Petal Power:* Ms. Martinez is the most beautiful bride in the world, and the sisters are there to help her get married. When trouble strikes her honeymoon plans, Tess and Erin must find a way to help save them.

#9 *First Place:* The Coronado Club insists Tess won't be able to hike across the Grand Canyon and plans to tell the whole sixth grade about it at Outdoor School. Tess looks confident but worries in silence, not wanting to share the secret that could lead to disaster.

#10 *Camp Cowgirl:* The Secret Sisters are ready for an awesome summer camp at a Tucson horse ranch, until something—and someone—interferes. What happens if your best friend wants other friends, and you're not sure, but you might too?

#11 *Picture Perfect:* Tess and Erin sign up for modeling school, but will they be able to go? Could they ever get any modeling assignments? Along the way the Secret Sisters find out that things aren't always just as they seem, a fact confirmed when Tess's mother has her baby.

#12 *Indian Summer:* When Tess and Erin sign up to go on their first mission trip—to the Navajo reservation—they plan to teach Vacation Bible School. What do a young Navajo girl and Tess have in common? In the end Tess has to make some of the most important choices in her new Christian life.

The Secret Sister Handbook: 101 Cool Ideas for You and Your Best Friend! It's fun to read about Tess and Erin and just as fun to do things with your own Secret Sister! This book is jam-packed with great things for you to do together all year long.